I could almost taste the salt spi
swept me away to another place and another time. This is
historical fiction at its best: gripping, well-researched,
spiritually solid, and with equal appeal to boys and girls.
I can't wait to read the next one!

> Robet Elmer
> Author of the Young Underground
> and Promise of Zion series

Page-turning adventure on the high seas! Both entertain-
ing and educational, *Raiders from the Sea* is a compelling
read. Not to be missed!

> Beverly Lewis
> Author of the Girls Only
> and SummerHill Secrets series

VIKING QUEST book one

RAIDERS
from the SEA

LOIS WALFRID JOHNSON

MOODY PUBLISHERS
CHICAGO

Glendalough is a real place—an Irish monastery that grew from the inspiration of St. Kevin in the 6th century. I've described Glendalough as it was in the late 900's. But with the exception of St. Kevin, all names and characters, including Brother Cronan, Bree, Devin, their family, and friends are fictitious. Any resemblance to persons living or dead is coincidental.

All Scripture quotations, unless otherwise indicated, are taken from the *Holy Bible, New International Version®*. NIV®. Copyright © 1973, 1978, 1984 by International Bible Society. Used by permission of Zondervan Publishing House. All rights reserved.

Published in association with the literary agency of Alive Communications, Inc., 7680 Goddard Street, Suite 200, Colorado Springs, Colorado 80920.

ISBN: 0-8024-3112-7

1 3 5 7 9 10 8 6 4 2

Printed in the United States of America

To Elaine—
Thank you
for encouraging the dream,
and then
walking the mountains
and seashores with me.

CONTENTS

INTRODUCTION

Today exciting explorations take us to the mysteries of outer space and wonders deep in the sea. In the days of the Vikings awesome adventures, including their discovery of the New World, lay just beyond the horizon. Yet whatever the time, something remains the same—young people like you with big dreams, the curiosity for adventure, and warm, courageous hearts.

HIDDEN THREAT

Without making a sound, Briana O'Toole slipped out the door to walk the mountain behind her home. In the half-light before dawn her reddish blonde hair swirled around her face. Her brown eyes peered into the mist that hid the valley below.

From the time she was born, Bree had lived in the Wicklow Mountains of Ireland. As if they were close friends, she knew every bush, tree, and stone along the path. What she *didn't* know was that this September day in the late tenth century marked the end of her old life and a new beginning.

After a steep climb, Bree reached her favorite spot on the side of Brockagh Mountain. When the breeze came, she felt it first upon her face. Moments later, the rising sun broke through the mist. The distant waters of the Irish Sea drew Bree in a way she couldn't explain even to herself. *If only I could know what's out there.*

For Bree the thought was not new. Years ago it started as a hunger—a curiosity that built with each story she heard about life in distant places. By now her wish to know the world beyond Ireland was a longing that wouldn't go away. What would it be like to see faraway lands?

Still watching the sea, Bree felt the dream of adventure. Then a whisper of fear crept into her thoughts. *Would I have the courage I'd need?*

Her brother, Devin, seemed brave enough for most anything. But Bree knew an unknown world might be frightening too. Whenever friends gathered in the cottages of Ireland, she heard stories about Vikings and their fast ships with the dragon heads. Fierce raiders from the North countries, they fell like lightning upon a peaceful countryside.

Bree shivered. *Please, God, not here. Not ever again.*

As the red ball of light grew large, the sun glittered and danced on the sea. Tossing her long hair over her shoulders, Bree shrugged off her worry. She'd let nothing spoil the wonder of this, her thirteenth birthday. In a loose-fitting blue dress that gave her the freedom to climb steep hills, Bree felt ready to celebrate.

When she started down the mountain, the mist still hung in the valleys, but she took the long way home. Even without seeing them, Bree knew every turn of the rivers that passed near her family's farm on their way to the Irish Sea.

Below her lay the place where she took her younger brother and sisters swimming. Beyond that sheltered spot, two rivers flowed together. Close by, her father had nearly drowned as a child. Often he warned them about the stepping-stones just upstream.

"People think it's an easy spot to cross," Daddy said. "But if something goes wrong—"

More than once, he had told Bree what to do if the younger children ever needed help. Always Bree felt glad for the way her dad praised her ability to swim. But now she felt the sun on her face and welcomed its warmth in her thoughts.

Someday I'll travel beyond these mountains, she promised herself. *Someday I'll see the world beyond the Irish Sea.*

In that moment the mist parted, showing Bree the place where the current ran swift and deep. There on the stepping-stones just above the joining of rivers was a lad with blond hair. *Tully!*

The boy stood on a rock with his back turned, but Bree felt sure she would recognize him anywhere. Wearing long narrow trousers and a sleeveless tunic, Tully was the son of her daddy's best friend. But what was he doing here, so far from home?

Bree's heart leaped just thinking about it. *Has Tully come to give me a birthday surprise?*

It would be just like her mother to plan something special with the Byrne family. But Bree couldn't wait. Moving on silent cat feet, she hurried down the hill, planning a surprise of her own.

On that September day the river ran full from autumn rains. Swirling water covered the stepping-stones on the far side of the river. As Tully moved from one stone to the next, Bree's excitement about a birthday surprise changed to uneasiness. *Can't he see how swift the current is?*

When he reached the last big stone, ready to slip into the water and swim the rest of the way, Bree called a warning. "Tully!"

At the sound of her voice he started to turn. Suddenly his foot slipped, and he lost his balance. Arms waving, he tumbled into the water.

On bare feet Bree raced to the edge of the river and followed the stones into the stream. There she found her worst fears true. Tully had hit his head when he fell. He lay facedown just beneath the surface of the water.

Dropping onto the closest stone, Bree stretched out. In that instant the current caught the still body and washed it beyond reach.

Filled with terror, Bree stood up and leaped into the river. With quick, powerful strokes she swam through the water. The moment she saw Tully's head, she reached down, caught his hair, and pulled him up. One hand under his arm and the other treading water, she kicked. When they broke the surface, she held up his head and kept kicking.

With one arm across his chest and swimming with the other, Bree started for shore. She had only one thought—getting Tully to breathe. But in that moment the full force of the current caught her. The powerful rush of water took them downstream.

Go with the current, Daddy had taught her. *Don't fight it. Let it carry you toward shore.* But time for Tully was running out. Her panic growing, Bree looked around for help.

The surrounding countryside lay empty, even of sheep. And now Bree faced another fear. How long could she hold him up?

Then, just as she started slipping under the water, she felt the river bottom. Setting down her feet, she found firm ground and headed for shore. With her last ounce of strength she dragged Tully onto a broad, flat rock.

As he lay on his stomach, Bree turned his face to one side and pounded his back. When Tully gagged, water poured from his mouth. Coughing, he started to breathe.

Relief stronger than any current poured through Bree. *He'll live!*

Then the boy raised his head. For the first time Bree caught a good look at his face. *It isn't Tully!*

A ripple of shock washed through her. *If it's not Tully, who is it?*

A red bruise on the boy's forehead marked the spot where he hit his head. Now his gasps for air became long gulps. Turning his head toward Bree, he muttered two words she didn't understand.

Puzzled, Bree watched the boy. Still catching her breath, she dropped down on the grassy bank next to him. Even her knees felt weak. Never had she felt so glad to touch the green sod of Ireland. Who could the boy possibly be?

On this side of the river, grass and stones gave way to steep hills. In the brief time they had been in the water, the sun had disappeared. A cloud of mist drifted between the mountains.

As though feeling the change in air, the boy rolled over and sat up. He seemed close to Bree's age, but the sun had given him a deep tan. His blond hair hung in a loose cut just below his ears. Most of all, Bree noticed his strong square jaw. Whoever this stranger was, she felt sure he wouldn't be afraid to express his opinions. But now his blue eyes looked confused.

"What happened?" he asked.

"You fell and hit your head."

"Where am I?"

"On a river that flows to the Irish Sea."

"Who are you?" the boy asked.

He spoke in Norse, a language used by traders, and Bree answered the same way. Her father, a great Irish chieftain, was also a merchant who traded with people from other lands. From the time Bree and her older brother were little, their daddy had taught them to speak Norse.

Instead of giving her name, Bree jumped up. "There's a spring nearby. I'll get you water." Moving quickly up the hill, Bree reached the spring and found the clay cup left for any passerby. Filling it with water, she returned to the boy.

"Thank you," he said when he had drunk deeply.

Bree only nodded. She was angry now—angry at the danger this boy had caused. "What were you doing, crossing there when the river runs so high?"

"I could have made it."

Bree couldn't believe her ears. "Don't you understand what happened?"

"I'm a strong swimmer."

"You hit your head." Bree's voice curled around her words. "You weren't breathing."

When his angry gaze met hers, Bree's temper flared. "You would have drowned without me!"

"I swim every day."

The blue eyes had changed. *Not so confused*, Bree told herself, glad that he seemed to be returning to normal. But his voice held a swagger that upset Bree even more.

Watching him closely, Bree understood why she had thought the boy was Tully. The same blond hair and blue eyes. The same look of knowing what they want and going straight toward it. But there the similarity ended.

What is it? Bree asked herself. Then she knew. While Tully was always kind to her family, the look of this stranger was sharp, almost cold. Even now, after nearly drowning, he wore a prideful air.

"So where do you do all this swimming you're so proud of?" Bree asked.

For an instant the stranger didn't speak, as though thinking about his answer. Then his words came in a rush. "Around my home."

"And where is your home?" Bree had lived near the river all her life. She had never seen the stranger.

Like a shifting shadow, something flitted through the boy's eyes. Turning toward the river, he tipped his head downstream. "That way."

Watching him, Bree felt uneasy. "What do you mean, *that way?* Down by the sea?"

"And beyond," he said.

Bree knew a stone wall had gone up between them. He was avoiding her questions. Upset now, she pounced. "What are you trying to hide?"

"Hide?" He looked innocent, but he reminded Bree of a boy she knew who didn't tell the truth.

"What's your name?" she asked.

"Michael," he told her.

Michael. Instantly Bree remembered a story in the Bible. When a courageous man named Daniel fasted and prayed, a high-ranking angel named Michael came to help him. But there was something about the way this Michael said his name. It bothered Bree. What was it?

I'm just jumpy, Bree told herself. As she started to ask more questions, the boy shivered. In the changing air Bree felt the cold. Though Michael also had good reason to be cold, she watched him closely.

His next shiver looked real. Grasping his upper arms, he hugged himself against the wind. "Do you have a blanket?" he asked. "Any food?"

Bree jumped to her feet. When she was only a young child her mother had taught her the Irish way. Countless times, Bree had seen her mother offer food, water, and shelter. "Sure, and it's the Lord Himself that we serve," she'd always say. But now a thought flashed through Bree's mind. *Whoever this lad is, I don't want to invite him home.*

"My mother will loan you some dry clothes," she told Michael.

Even as she spoke, Bree kept watching him. The boy couldn't be much older than she, but he seemed more grown-up. More sure of himself. Bree wondered about it.

Then her family's habit of hospitality won out. "I'll get you something to eat."

Michael nodded. He trembled now, and his teeth chattered.

Walking quickly, Bree crossed a nearby pasture and climbed over a stone wall. Beyond were a grass-covered hill and then the oak forest. Partway up the hill, Bree suddenly changed direction. Not even to herself could she explain why.

Instead of taking the shortest route home, Bree headed for a rise where trees grew close together. When she reached a place where she could slip out of sight, she looked back.

Michael still sat at the edge of the river, huddled against the cold. Even from where she stood, Bree saw the trembling in his shoulders. He had turned to watch which way she went.

Raising an arm, he waved. In that moment Michael seemed just another boy about her age. For the first time Bree felt sorry for him. He would have been better off walking fast with her. At least he would have stayed warm. But Bree still felt uneasy and wasn't willing to ignore that warning.

The moment the trees hid her, she changed direction again. As she climbed the steep hill at the bottom of Brockagh Mountain, she felt grateful for her strong body. Just last week her brother Devin had told her, "Bree, you've kept up to me all your life. You don't have to do everything I do."

"Yes, I do," Bree had answered. But even to this brother

she loved, Bree couldn't explain why. Always she had known that she needed to be physically strong, able to climb mountains without panting for breath. Able to walk long distances and swim in cold water. This morning had proved it.

Moving quickly between the oaks, Bree doubled back onto the shortest route home. Soon she dropped down to a meadow. Sheep grazed there, looking so peaceful that for the first time ever, they seemed out of place.

By the time Bree reached her family's farm, she decided she had imagined all her reasons for questions. Inside the house, she snatched up dry clothes and a blanket. In the kitchen she gathered a loaf of bread and a small pail of milk. As she headed back out the door, she nearly crashed into her older brother.

Slender and tall for his age, Devin stood straight as an arrow and had their father's black hair and deep blue eyes. A year older than Bree, Devin was the one who shortened her name. Using the Irish word for a high, rocky hill, he often told her, "When you're stubborn, you're like a mountain that can't be moved."

Her brother meant to tease, but Bree liked having a name that reminded her of the lofty headland up the coast from where they lived. For as long as she could remember, Devin had watched out for her. Usually Bree didn't appreciate his help. Now he wanted to know what she was doing.

"I saved a lad from drowning," Bree said.

"Drowning?" Devin's blue eyes widened. "Where?"

"You know the stepping-stones where the rivers come together? Where we never swim because of the current?"

"So you swam there? Dad won't like that!"

"If I hadn't, the boy would have drowned. He hit his head when he fell."

As Bree started back across the meadow, Devin took the bread and pail of milk and followed. "So now you're bringing him this?"

"He's tired. Too tired and cold to come here."

Still wondering if she were imagining things, Bree didn't explain her mixed-up feelings. She and Devin walked quickly without taking time to talk. When they reached the high place overlooking the river, Bree glanced ahead and stopped short.

"Where is he?" Devin asked.

Bree shrugged. "Maybe he's behind a bush or tree. Staying out of the wind."

Worried now, she broke into a run. But when she reached the rock where Michael had been, there was no one in sight.

"You're sure you have the right place?" Devin asked.

"I'm sure."

"So where is he, this lad you rescued?"

With growing uneasiness, Bree dropped the blanket and started downstream. In one spot she leaped from rock to rock. Whenever she reached an open place, she looked around. Finally she changed direction, hurried back to Devin, and followed the river upstream.

At last Bree had to give up. Whoever the boy was, he was nowhere to be found.

When she again returned to her brother, Bree saw the look in his eyes. "You're sure you didn't imagine things?" he asked.

Bree shook her head. She had no doubt that she had saved a boy from drowning. Besides, her dress and long, reddish blonde hair were only partly dry. But where could Michael be? Though he didn't want to admit it, he needed help.

Or did he? Uneasy nudges poked at Bree's thoughts. *Yes, he had almost drowned. But after that? Did he just pretend he was cold?* It all seemed so strange.

Now Devin turned on her. "Did you really swim here by yourself? Are you trying to cover up so I don't tell Dad?"

"Daddy nearly drowned here as a boy," Bree told him. "He told me what to do if I ever needed to help."

"But if you helped a lad, where is he?" Devin asked for the third time.

Even to Bree, it didn't seem real. How could Michael just disappear?

Then she looked down. One flat rock next to the river was still wet. Bree pointed to it. "That's where I helped him out."

The whole thing worried Bree. Michael had avoided her questions. Bree felt sure of that. But was he dizzy and mixed up from hitting his head? Did he fall into the river and drown after all?

Filled with misery, Bree stared upstream and down. It was all her fault. He was cold and weak, and she shouldn't have left him.

"What was the boy's name?" Devin asked, still curious.

"Michael." Bree spoke slowly. "He said his name was Michael. You know like the angel in the Bible?"

In that instant Bree understood why she felt uneasy. "But he pronounced *Michael* a different way."

Suddenly Bree felt angry. *It wasn't Michael who needed help. It was me.*

Not even to this brother who cared about her did Bree want to admit her questions. *I found Michael here in early morning. Did he come as a spy in the night? Did I catch him off guard because he thought no one was around?*

Deep inside, Bree started to tremble. *Who is this boy who seems to know exactly what he plans to do?*

THE WARNING

Then Bree knew she had no choice but to speak. As though the strange boy was hidden nearby, she lowered her voice. "You know how we say the name for Michael the angel?"

"*Meehaul.*" Devin looked troubled.

"And you know the way we learn a language?" Bree and Devin were learning Latin from Brother Cronan, a monk at the school near their home. Often he asked them to repeat an unknown word until they pronounced it exactly right.

In the dark days when barbarians invaded the European continent, students from many lands had fled to Ireland and the monastery at Glendalough (pronounced

Glen-da-loch). Often Bree felt proud that she could study there. Other times she wanted to give up because Brother Cronan expected so much of her. But always her curiosity kept Bree going.

Now she knew something that put that curiosity to good use. "The boy I rescued gave his name as though he heard an Irishman say Michael," she said. "But there was a difference—a little twist on the word."

"There's something more." Devin spoke slowly, as if still thinking. "Do you know a single Irish child named Michael?"

Bree understood what he meant. "It's a name we respect."

"Respect so much that parents don't name their children Michael," Devin said. "Someday they probably will. But in the Bible Michael isn't just any angel. He's a mighty prince who fought against the king of Persia."

Trying to push down her panic, Bree drew a deep breath.

"What else is wrong?" Devin asked.

"We talked Norse together."

"A lot of people know Norse." Devin sounded as if he was trying to shrug it off. "Maybe his father is a trader like ours. Or maybe he's a new student at school—just someone we don't know."

The monastery school had grown large, and Devin could easily be right. But his blue eyes looked worried, and there was something Bree couldn't ignore. Long ago, Viking raiders had discovered the wealth of monasteries in Ireland and other countries.

"We live so close to Glendalough," Bree said. "So close to the gold and precious gems that pilgrims bring to the monastery. What if——?" She stopped.

"What if what?"

No longer could Bree push aside her fear. "I found the boy here soon after sunrise. What if he came during the night to spy out the land?"

Even the memory of those moments set Bree's heart beating faster. "Dev, I'm scared. Could the boy be a Viking?"

For a minute her brother didn't answer. Then he said, "We have to warn Mam and Dad."

Bree stared at him. *This is the brother who is always brave.* More than once Bree had wished she had his courage. Devin never gave something a second thought unless there was good reason to be worried. Now he looked more upset than she had seen him in years.

"You're sure?" Bree asked. "What if I'm just imagining things?" If they didn't tell anyone about the strange boy, maybe their worries would vanish.

But when Devin spoke, his voice was harsh. "We didn't imagine things when Vikings took Keely away."

Bree blinked, but her tears came anyway. Their sister Keely had been the youngest girl in the family the last time Vikings came. On that day, life had changed forever for the O'Toole family.

Bree struggled to speak. "Do you think we'll ever see Keely again?"

"I hope so."

Bree saw the pain in his eyes, but Devin surprised her with a quick brotherly hug. "Whoever that boy is, what happened isn't your fault. How could you know that he's a Viking? We still don't know. We can only guess."

As much as Bree wanted to believe everything would be all right, she agreed with Devin. They couldn't take a chance. "You go home," she said. "I'll go to the monastery."

Long ago, Bree and Devin had discovered the short-est path from this part of the river to their farm. As young children, they made a game of it, racing to see who reached home first. But their father had warned them. "Keep changing the way you take so you don't beat down a path to our door."

By this time Bree and Devin knew several routes, all of them unmarked. Partway up the hill, Devin turned toward the farm while Bree kept on through the forest. When she reached a place overlooking Glendalough, she paused to catch her breath.

Below her lay the monastery that grew from the inspiration of St. Kevin in the sixth century. By now, late in the tenth century, thousands of people had come to county Wicklow and the monastery whose name meant the Valley of Two Lakes.

With its many buildings, Glendalough was called a monastic city. Men, women, and children lived and worked inside the protection of its walls. And here was the school that offered daily teaching. While many students became lifelong monks, others such as Bree and Devin were just there to learn.

And I live close enough to come! To Bree it seemed a miracle that she could read and write Latin, the language of the Bible. As a young child she had often pestered her brother about what he studied. Each evening, after Bree spent the day learning how to keep house, Devin taught her what he had learned. Finally he had grown tired of her questions.

When he couldn't give an answer, Devin glared at her. "Why don't you ask Brother Cronan yourself?"

Bree smiled. "Well, of course, I will."

Devin had looked worried. "Oh, no, Bree! I didn't mean *that*."

"Well, I do. If he and the other monks can teach students from all over Ireland and Europe, why can't they teach someone living right here?"

"They do. Me."

"But why can't they teach a girl?"

"Look, I've helped you learn," Devin had answered. "I didn't mean to cause trouble."

Bree grinned. "You didn't. You just gave me an idea. The monks teach noblemen, but they also teach commoners. And the men of Ireland honor their women."

When Devin grinned, Bree hurried on. "Sure, and if Ireland doesn't have her share of famous women. Warriors and rulers and poets—think about all the Irish women who have done heroic things."

"Women, Bree. That's the word. Not girls—*colleens* like you."

Bree had hooted with laughter. Then she'd straightened her face and spoke in her most serious voice. "Women start out as girls."

Caught in the joke, Devin had laughed too.

Bree seized the moment. "I could go to school with you!" They were friends as well as brother and sister. She would like that. "I could keep up with you. I know I could."

"That's what I'm afraid of." Devin had become serious then. "You'd make life hard for me."

But Bree wasn't one to wait on an idea. The moment she thought of something, she did her best to carry it out. "I'm going to ask Brother Cronan."

In charge of the school at Glendalough, Cronan was also a scribe who copied the Bible. When Bree first saw those pages, she felt drawn to the bright colors. Before long, she understood why the monks felt it so important to make handwritten copies of the sacred words. Bree's desire to be a good reader became a longing to know the Bible for herself.

Now, still full of questions about the lad she had rescued from drowning, Bree hurried to the stone arch in the high walls of Glendalough. The gatekeeper knew Bree and waved her on.

Usually she stopped at St. Kevin's cross, but today Bree hurried to the tower that rose far above the other buildings. More than ninety-eight feet high, its round stone walls were over three feet thick at the bottom. Five of the seven levels had one small window. The four windows on the top floor each faced a different way.

Always Bree had taken those windows for granted. Now she thought about them. A lookout could see in every direction.

Bree knew that monks called people to church by ringing a handbell from those top windows. She also felt sure that monks went to the tower to pray and that Cronan used the tower to hide monastery treasures. But today she could imagine still another use.

Looking up at the tall, cone-shaped building, Bree stared at the door over thirteen feet above the ground. If raiders from the sea crept through the forest, the tower could be a hiding place for anyone who ran there for safety. Once inside, they could pull up the ladder and bar the door.

After all that had happened at the river, Bree needed that thought. But she couldn't forget the hard look in

Michael's eyes. Wanting to feel safe, Bree stretched out her hand toward the tower. In the next moment she changed her mind.

Turning around, she walked back to St. Kevin's cross. There, standing before the cross carved from one large granite stone, Bree looked up and started to pray. *Lord, You know that I'm scared right down to my toes. Whatever happens to me—whatever happens in my life—will You help me know that You're always with me?*

Once more Bree headed for the building where scribes made handwritten copies of the Bible. Just inside the doorway of the room she loved best, a monk was making the bright ink that decorated special books.

Brother Cronan sat on a high stool in a corner. His long hair fell away from the shaved part of his head. His brown robe hung to the floor around his sandaled feet. With a steady pen he wrote on the vellum, or calfskin, that was used for honored books such as the Bible.

Bree stood back to not disturb her teacher yet be able to see every stroke of his pen. Cronan was a gifted artist in the way he copied the Holy Scriptures. As Bree watched, he filled the first letter of the gospel of John with bright colors and a complicated design. Afraid that she would spoil his work, Bree waited until Cronan turned to her.

When he did, a warm smile lit his face. "How are you, Briana?" he asked as he had on that long-ago day when Bree first met him. "Remember how you came here on your ninth birthday?"

Startled, Bree nodded. With the number of students he had, how did he manage to think of something like that? But that's the way it was with Brother Cronan.

"Happy birthday, child," he said now, as he had then.

Bree blinked. With the dangers of the morning, she had forgotten about her birthday.

"You stood behind me just as you did now. I saw the same wonder in your face—an awe for the Holy Scriptures."

Moved by his kindness, Bree stood there, not knowing what to say. Cronan went on. "I've been thinking about you this morning. In fact, I've been praying for you as I worked. Is something wrong?"

When Bree couldn't answer, she nodded. As though she was still down by the river, she saw the prideful boy named Michael, and she shivered.

The monk set down his pen and stood up, but his gaze never left her face. "What is it, child?"

Her teacher's kindness was more than Bree could handle. She had to swallow twice but finally got the words out. "I need to warn you."

Instantly the monk's smile disappeared.

"I think you'll want to talk to Daddy," Bree told him. "Devin says it's important."

"Then it must be. Devin never makes a mistake on something like that. He's a born leader."

A smile returned to the monk's eyes. "And it's meal-time. It's important that I know whether your mam is still a good cook."

With Cronan walking quickly and Bree following close behind, they soon covered the distance between the monastery and the farm. When they reached the house, they found the O'Toole family ready to sit down for their midday meal.

Bree's mother, Maureen, put another plate on the table and quickly added to the light meal they usually had at noon. Soon the aroma of roasting meat and freshly baked bread filled the cottage.

More than once, people had told Bree that she had both the reddish blonde hair and the warm smile of her mother. But now when Mam invited the monk to eat with them, Devin was impatient of the delay.

"Did you tell Brother Cronan what happened?" he whispered to Bree. "What did he say?"

Bree shrugged, shook her head, and looked around. At one side of the large open room was the cooking fire. Daddy had made Bree's grandmother a bed near its warmth, for she was cold much of the time. Her place in the midst of them helped her take part in their lives. With bright, perky eyes, she spoke to the children whenever they passed near her.

Now Bree's father stepped forward. With a warm welcome, Aidan O'Toole drew his friend Cronan over to the table. Bree's seven-year-old brother, Adam, and her younger sisters, Cara and Jen, sat down between Bree and her mother.

"You're just as good a cook as ever, Maureen," Cronan said halfway through the meal.

Mam smiled with pleasure. The compliment always pleased her. All of southeastern Ireland knew about the cooking skills of Maureen O'Toole. Whatever she prepared proved tasty, and she was making sure that Bree became just as good a cook.

Today Cronan surprised Bree by eating quickly. When he finished his last forkful, he looked toward Adam, Cara, and Jen. Bree's father caught the signal.

"Go outside, children," he told them. "But stay close to the house."

As soon as they left, Cronan spoke. "Briana tells me there's something I need to know. Now, child, tell us why you and Devin feel I need to be warned."

With a trembling heart, Bree began the story of the strange boy who didn't know how to pronounce his own name.

THREE

BREE'S BIRTHDAY

As Bree talked, she watched her father. At first a thundercloud passed over his face. Bree knew that Daddy had all he could do to hold in his anger about what might happen if raiders returned to their area.

Two hundred years before, Vikings had begun their raids along the seacoasts of Ireland and Scotland. Forty-six years later, in 841, Viking merchants established a trading base at Dublin. By now, in the late 900s, Vikings had raided the Glendalough monastery many times.

Today her father listened without taking his eyes off Bree for a second. When he asked a question, she did her best to remember every detail.

Devin remained silent, seeming to listen for anything

Bree might miss. When she finished, her mother's face was white and still, her eyes filled with dread.

Cronan spoke quietly. "We've had peace for a time, but we cannot have a false peace. Briana, we need this warning so we're always ready at Glendalough. As the Vikings have come before, they will probably come again."

Like a thick fog closing in on them, the word *Viking* hung in the air. Fierce men who swooped down on monasteries and nearby homes, they struck at a moment's notice. With the shallow draft of their longships they were able to enter rivers and streams. Often they appeared far from the sea where no one expected them.

Until this moment Bree had managed to push aside her worst fears. No longer could she ignore them.

From her earliest memory, she had looked to her father whenever something went wrong. Now the deep blue eyes of Aidan O'Toole were dark with concern. Yet when he spoke, his voice held the strength of a good leader. Already he had a plan.

"We must remind everyone of the danger," he said. "Sometimes people forget the burning and looting of times past. The signal—the monastery bell—our people must remember is that one kind of ring calls them to church. Another way of ringing says, 'Flee! Go to your hiding place.'"

His glance took in Devin. "Put fresh buckets of water

in the places we've prepared. Also take the warm blankets we use in winter, and food that can be stored for a time."

To Bree he said, "I want you and Devin to make sure that everything is ready. We've given you the safest place we have, but it's also the smallest. Use every inch of space wisely."

Daddy looked toward the cooking fire. In spite of its warmth, Granny lay like a small bird in a nest of blankets. Awake one moment, she dozed the next. She was the reason why Bree and Devin were in charge of the younger children.

Then Daddy turned to Mam. "Maureen, my love, if I'm home when raiders come, we'll work together. If I'm not, take Granny and go. If you don't have time for the animals, just take care of yourselves."

When Bree's father turned to the monk, the gaze of the two friends met across the table. "You've already prepared a safe place for the monks and students."

"The tower stands ready," Cronan answered.

"And the manuscripts? Do you need our help?"

"We'll finish hiding them so that no one—*no one*—can find them."

"The manuscripts?" Bree whispered. With their beautiful colors, the hand-copied pages of the Bible seemed to have light shining through them. She couldn't think of anything worse than having them stolen.

Cronan nodded. "The raiders don't understand why

the Bible means so much to us. They worship pagan gods and steal our Bibles because of the precious gems on the covers."

Once again the monk spoke to Bree's father. "I'll leave some things out where they can find them—treasures that aren't so valuable and manuscripts we've just begun. We'll try to give the Vikings enough so they don't keep searching for more."

Daddy seemed to feel satisfied that they had planned every way they could. But when Mam spoke, her voice was so changed that Bree barely recognized it. "Can we pray?" she asked.

"Yes, certainly." For an instant Cronan looked around the table. His gaze paused at the three empty plates, as though thinking of Adam, Cara, and Jen. Then he spoke to Devin. "You're a born leader, just like your father. God will use your many gifts."

His eyes solemn, Devin nodded. "Thank you."

The monk turned to Bree's father and mother. "We need to continue teaching the children to trust the Lord, no matter what happens. Let's especially encourage Briana."

"Especially?" Mam's voice was faint. "Oh, no, Cronan, no!" In the next instant she clapped her hands over her mouth, as though trying to shut off her words. But the frightened look remained in her eyes.

After a silence that seemed to last forever, Cronan

bowed his head and prayed. "Lord, deliver us from the wrath of the men from the North. Good and kind Lord, protect us all."

Bree's silent prayer echoed his. *And, Lord, protect us from that hateful boy, whoever he is.*

When the monk left, Bree, Devin, and their parents returned to the table. Bree always loved the rumble of her daddy's big laugh, but he wasn't laughing today.

Bree's gaze met her father's solemn blue eyes. "Do you remember when I asked Brother Cronan if I could start school? Ever since he came to talk with you, you've offered his prayer for protection. And you've taught us what to do."

Now Bree was old enough to understand that Daddy had given her and Devin a carefully laid-out plan to take the younger children to the forest. "You made it a game. We didn't know how important that game might become."

"Until now." Devin looked from one to the other. "Until today. Down by the stepping-stones in the river. We talked about Keely again."

Whenever their sister's name came up, Bree saw the pain in her mother and father. The loss had left Mam a quieter woman, Daddy a more thoughtful man. Often Bree caught their gaze resting on the youngest children. God had given her parents a second family.

But now Bree could only think about the days ahead.

What's going to happen to us? she wondered, her heart filled with dread. *What will happen to my family and me?*

Sad, angry, and scared all at once, Bree tried to push down her feelings. Instead, they spilled over into words. "I don't want to be afraid."

Her daddy reached out and put his large hand over hers. "We all have times when we're afraid," he said.

"You too?" The idea startled Bree.

"There's nothing wrong with being afraid. Sometimes that's God's way of protecting us."

Tears filled her father's eyes. "My daughter—" He swallowed hard and blinked the tears away. "Briana—" Again he needed to stop.

The way Daddy spoke her name made Bree feel better. From the time she was a little girl she had sensed his care for her mother and each child in the family. Her father's way of loving all of them gave Bree a warm feeling of being watched over.

Now he went on. "There will always be people who try to defeat us. If we let them frighten us, they win. But do you know what? Sometimes we do the biggest things —the most important things—when we're afraid. What counts is how we live, even though we're scared."

As though wanting to be sure she understood, her father leaned forward. "Briana, you have learned the Holy Scriptures—stored them in your heart. They will be a comfort to you."

Stunned, Bree waited for Daddy to say more, but he didn't. "A comfort to *me?*" she asked, barely able to speak. If there was a need for comfort, it meant that something bad had happened. Something was hard, or dangerous, or frightening.

"The Word of God will be like a sword that helps you defeat your enemies."

Bree didn't want to think about possible enemies. Some time before, her father had fallen away from God and left the church. Bree was awake the night she heard him sobbing, asking the Lord to forgive him. From that time on, Aidan O'Toole had been a changed man. Now he spoke truth, and Bree knew it. With every part of her being she wanted to cry out, "There will be no need for comfort!"

Then her father spoke straight into her heart. "Briana, if a test comes, remember how much we love you. And know that you'll have the courage to win."

"But how?" Bree asked. Then she remembered. Long ago Daddy had started talking to her and Devin about the courage to win. "You think I'd have the courage for something *really* hard?"

Her father smiled. "Come here," he said. "I want to give you a hug so you remember."

When Bree stood next to him, she felt like a little girl instead of thirteen years old. Her father reached out his arm and circled her with his love. "Happy birthday,

Briana," he said gently. "I want you to always remember this day."

Remember? Bree could do that. After all, it was her birthday.

"And remember this," her father went on. "Whatever you face, if you ask God to help you, He will."

FOREST HIDEAWAY

The green hills of Ireland were soft with evening mist when Devin O'Toole reached the river. Upstream from where Bree rescued the boy named Michael, the river flowed alongside the family farm. After a quick glance in all directions, Devin slipped under the trailing branches of a tall willow.

Turning, he looked back to check on his sister Bree. She, too, carried a heavy load of dried fish and grains. Strapped to her back, as well as Devin's, was a wooden container filled with water. If they needed to stay in the shelter for a time, they would be well supplied until they could get water from a spring. Balancing the weight of their supplies, Devin loaded their rowboat.

It took two more trips to the house before he and Bree had everything they needed. When all was ready, Bree stepped in and Devin pushed out from shore. Each of them taking an oar, they sent the boat skimming across the water.

For years they had practiced, first for fun, then to see how quickly they could row upstream. Devin felt proud of the way he and Bree worked together.

"We're good at this," he said, keeping his voice soft. "We're sure to escape any enemy that comes."

But then Bree turned toward him. Devin caught the look in her face. Bree's eyes were the deep brown of the deer that roamed their forest, and Devin had learned to read his sister's feelings. She was more scared than she wanted to admit.

Bree had been unusually quiet since their midday meal. "What did the stranger look like?" Devin asked.

"Like our good friend Tully." Bree spit out the words.

Devin could only guess the terror Bree had felt. First to see someone she thought was a friend nearly drown. Then instead of a Byrne, she had saved a possible enemy.

Silently dipping their oars, Devin and Bree made good time against the current. As they rowed, Devin studied the shoreline and reminded himself of every marker. A noticeable rock here. A tall oak there. An unusual turn in the shoreline or a bit of land that crept out in the water. If they came this way at night, he must be able to recognize where they were. At any moment they might need to seek refuge along the river.

When they passed three pines growing close to the riverbank, Devin remembered his need to teach Bree. "That could be a place to hide the boat."

His sister nodded. "But I hope we can reach the shelter."

Here and there Devin pointed out other important landmarks. "If Vikings come, they'll probably leave their ship down the river. From whatever direction they walk in, they can look down on the monastery."

When Bree shivered, Devin felt sure she had thought of the same thing.

As they rowed, the sun slipped behind the mountains, and the sound of falling water grew louder by the moment. Some distance downstream from a thundering waterfall, they came to the odd-shaped rock that was their marker. Reaching out, Devin grabbed hold and swung the boat alongside. Quickly he tied up to a tree on the shore. Working together, he and Bree unloaded the supplies and hid what they couldn't carry on their first trip.

The way between the rocks was steep. The path they followed was one of their own choosing. They had always been careful not to leave signs that would give them away. As they walked, Devin looked up often. Studying the trees, he thought about how they'd look if he and Bree passed that way at night.

Once a deer startled them by bounding out from a bush. Soon after, Devin found the marker he needed and walked straight toward it. There he stopped, looked around, and took a zigzag route to their hiding place.

Set inside a cluster of pines, the shelter blended into the thick growth around it. Sturdy branches held a horizontal pole in place. Leaning across that pole were several others that slanted down to the ground. Lodged between the roots of trees, they made a strong wall and roof. A straw thatch covered the poles to keep out the rain.

Devin and Bree set to work, stacking things carefully to give room for all of them. When their father first talked about making a place to hide, Cara was one year old and Jen newly born. "We'll build a shelter near one of our waterfalls," Dad had said.

At fourteen, Devin understood why. If either girl started to cry, she would betray everyone else. Here, the tumbling water would cover the sound. Here, too, the distance from the monastery might help keep them safe.

By now the shelter had a floor of beaten-down earth with a dry rug ready to spread across it. A blanket dropped down to close the doorway.

On the second trip from the rowboat, Bree led Devin to the hiding place. After still another trip, they had everything inside. "We're as ready as we can be," Devin said, trying to encourage her.

But when they returned to the river again, he felt

uneasy. "Let's find a better hiding place for the boat. If we're not careful, it could give us away."

With dusk gathering around them, he and Bree searched. After a time, they discovered a small opening between two large rocks. If they tied the rowboat so it didn't drift, it would be out of sight from the main channel.

Devin found a strong stick, pushed it into the riverbank, and showed Bree how to tie up the boat. "If we have time, we'll find another place," he said. "But I don't think they'll come this far." *They* had become their word for Vikings.

"Are you sure?" Bree asked. "Can anyone predict what Vikings will do?"

Devin didn't answer. He didn't want to even guess how difficult life could become. He only wanted to protect his brother and three sisters.

I'll keep them safe, he promised himself as he pushed down his fear. *Somehow I'll keep them safe—even if it's a matter of life or death.*

But now daylight was gone, and it was difficult to see rocks in the dark water. "Let's look again tomorrow," Devin said.

Heading downstream, they rode the current, needing to do little more than keep the rowboat in the center of the river. In that peaceful moment the strangeness of their plan and the terrible need behind it became real. As though a cold wind had come up, Bree shivered.

"What's the matter?" Devin asked.

Bree started to speak and then stopped. Devin sat close enough to see the side of her face. "Swallowing your words?" he asked, trying to make her feel better.

Bree shrugged, and Devin was afraid to share his own thoughts. Just the same, it felt good to be with his sister.

"I was thinking—" Bree started, then stopped again.

"Thinking." Devin offered a great sigh.

But Bree went on anyway. "You know what, Dev? You're a pretty good brother."

"You're sure?"

"Yes, I'm sure," Bree answered. "I guess I've never told you that before."

"Nope. You've never said anything that important."

"Well—" Bree looked uncomfortable. "I would tell Mam I love her, and I would tell Daddy. But it's pretty hard to tell you."

Devin felt embarrassed. "And it wouldn't enter my head to tell you." But something stirred inside him—an uneasiness he couldn't explain. "Just in case you ever need to know—if you ever start wondering what I think of you—"

"Sure." Bree choked with laughter, or so Devin thought. Then she turned to look at him. Again the moonlight gave her away. The tears were back in her eyes.

"You too," he said quietly.

"Me too?" she asked.

"You're a pretty good sister," was all he managed to say.

Then, like a flash of lightning, Devin had an idea so awful that he pushed it away. If he didn't think about it, maybe it wouldn't happen. But when Devin tried to ignore the thought, it became stronger.

He and Bree were like many brothers and sisters. Often they argued. Often they teased. Yet when there was something difficult outside their family, they fought it together, and usually they won. But now Devin asked himself, *What if we don't win this time?*

Like a warning the thought came. As far back as he could remember, Devin had watched out for Bree. But here was something new—something bigger than he might be able to handle. *What if the Vikings win?*

Without making a ripple, Devin dipped his oar, guiding the rowboat. From around them he heard the sound of running water. From the smaller waterfalls here and there throughout the forest came a quietness he had learned to recognize.

Usually Devin felt he wasn't much good at praying. After all, wasn't that what Brother Cronan was for? But Devin had learned to be still when the monk asked them to be silent and pray. Devin had seen that stillness when his father stopped whatever he was doing and seemed to listen for a moment. And Devin had learned to listen when he was afraid.

Now from deep within, he sensed words he didn't want to hear. *Help Bree for the time when she has to be alone.*

Devin's hands tightened on his oar. He tried to push the thought away, but it returned. Like a great sob, terror rose up inside him. *If Bree has to be alone, does it mean——?*

Devin wouldn't let himself finish the question. Instead, he remembered the talk at the table that noon. *Brother Cronan knew it. Dad knows it. And Mam too. God, do You sometimes warn us—to help us be ready for something hard?*

Around the river, the night sounds were soft. Devin could no longer push aside the thought he wanted to ignore. *Help Bree for the time when she is alone.*

This time he prayed. *How, Lord?*

As the boat glided downstream, he remembered. Long ago, a mean boy—a lad older than Devin—lived on the next farm. More than once, the boy had been cruel to both Devin and Bree. On the day he turned eight, Devin knew he had to stand up to him.

"We need a secret sign," Devin had told Bree. "A sign that helps me win."

Bree thought about it. "Mam says that Jesus wants to help us whenever we're scared."

"And Dad says we need to have courage," Devin answered.

"What's courage?" seven-year-old Bree had asked.

"Doing the right thing, even if I'm scared."

Bree thought for only a moment. "By yourself you're

just an ordinary boy. And I'm your ordinary sister. But if we ask God to help us—"

Bree crossed her arms over her chest. "When you see this, you'll know I'm praying for you."

Devin grinned. "It's a good sign—our secret sign."

"When I'm praying for you, you'll have courage to win."

Soon Devin learned that Bree was right. When he faced the mean boy from the next farm, Devin felt sure the lad would beat him up. But then he caught sight of Bree and her signal.

Standing as tall as possible, he remembered how Dad spoke when he expected someone to obey. Devin did the same. To his surprise the boy backed away and left him alone.

From that day on, Devin and Bree used their secret signal. When they didn't know what to do, they practiced asking God for help. There was a time when Devin had a high fever. For two days he was so sick that he didn't know where he was. Early one morning he looked up and saw Bree standing next to his bed.

Her eyes were scared, but she crossed her arms in their secret sign. "Courage to win, Dev," she whispered, then pointed to the ceiling. "Jesus helps us with everything."

The next time Devin woke, his fever was gone.

Sometimes when they used the signal, it seemed that Devin and Bree *didn't* win—not on the outside where they could see what happened. But always they won on the inside, where courage counted most.

Now Devin let his oar rest on his lap. When the moon rose above the trees, he pointed to the sky as they had done when they were little children. "Courage to win, Bree," he said quietly.

"Courage to win, Dev." Her smile was warm with remembering.

In the morning light Devin felt better. *Nothing really awful can happen on a day like this,* he told himself as he finished breakfast. As he watched his sisters, everything seemed as normal as always.

At one end of the large, open room, Bree stood before a mirror of highly polished metal. As she combed through her long wavy hair, the little girls watched every move she made.

Four-year-old Cara was always the most serious. Reaching out, she touched the cloth of Bree's bright blue dress. When Bree peered into the mirror, Cara tried to see herself in the reflection. Then, as Bree braided the long hair that fell down her back, Cara tried to do the same. Instead, her short curls escaped her fingers.

In contrast to Cara's red hair and freckles, Jen had their father's dark hair. "Why do you go to school?" she asked Bree now.

"I like to read books and find out about faraway lands," Bree told her.

"Faraway lands?" That was beyond the three-year-old.

"Places I've never been," Bree explained. "Places that aren't home."

"Oh." Jen's mouth formed a perfect circle. "I like home."

"I do too," Bree answered quickly. Years older than the little girls, she often acted like a mother to them.

As Devin watched, Bree tucked her comb and a small mirror into a bag she carried with her. *Finally!* he thought. *At last she is ready!*

When Devin and Bree left for school, Adam and the girls followed them out the door. As they started along the path to the river, Devin looked around the meadow. The morning sunlight felt warm with the memory of good times the family had shared while making hay.

Today, as always, the younger children walked with them as far as the stone wall. A gate shut them safely away from the river as it passed through their farm.

Jen talked nonstop all the way there. "Fish are happy in the river, aren't they?"

When Devin nodded, Jen's blue eyes shone. "Frogs like to croak, don't they?"

Across Jen's dark head, Devin grinned at Bree. Then Adam, Cara, and Jen waved until Devin and Bree reached the forest where they slipped out of sight.

That afternoon the Viking raiders came.

Bree had just returned from school when the monastery bell echoed across the mountain. Instantly she recognized the signal. *Run for your lives!*

RACE FOR LIFE

B ree froze. Like a giant wave of the sea, fear for her family washed over her. In that awful moment Bree could only feel glad that she was home.

Then with surprise she found that her feet would move after all. As she raced for the house, Devin ran from the barn. They met at the kitchen door. When Devin jerked it open, Bree put her hand on his arm. "We can't frighten them."

Devin took a deep breath and stepped inside. Bree followed him.

Cara and Jen sat at the kitchen table eating bread smeared with honey. Already Mam was helping Granny onto a small cart that would carry her into the forest.

"It's time for the game," Mam told the little girls. Her quiet voice surrounded all of them with her love. "Go along now, darlin's."

Mam's careful smile took in Devin, then lingered on Bree. Suddenly Mam stopped what she was doing, hurried over, and hugged Bree. "The Lord keep you," she said quickly, then, "Adam is outside."

Bree snatched up a towel and tied two loaves of bread inside its corners. Taking Jen's hand, Bree led her to the door. "First one to the boat wins!" she exclaimed, starting the game.

But then Bree turned, darted back, and planted a kiss on her mother's cheek. "Love you, Mam," she said. "Love you always."

Tears filled her mother's eyes. "Love you forever, Bree."

Outside, Devin had found Adam, but the seven-year-old was being stubborn.

"Take the girls," Bree told her older brother. With one in each arm he headed for the river.

"Adam, come!" Bree said. "You must obey."

"Don't feel like it. I'm tired."

Bree stopped and took a good look at him. Reaching down, she felt his forehead. *A fever!*

"But we've started our game." Bree held out her hand. "If you hurry, I'll give you a prize when we get in the boat."

Fighting for time, Bree pulled Adam along the path and through the gate to the river. By the time they reached Devin, he had the little girls sitting on the bottom of the boat.

Again Adam dug in his heels. Now he was unwilling to get in the boat. Tossing the bread at Devin, Bree picked up Adam. Angry now, he kicked her shins. Devin grabbed the boy's feet and Bree set him inside the boat. A moment later, Devin pushed off.

"I don't want to go!" Adam complained.

"Quiet now," Bree warned. "Your voice carries on the water."

"I don't care!"

"Part of the game is to be quiet," Bree told him.

"I want Mam," Adam answered. "I want Daddy!"

"Hush now!" Frantically Bree untied the towel, tore off a piece of bread, and thrust it into Adam's hand. That upset the girls.

"He didn't win!" Jen complained, wanting the special treatment Bree had promised.

"You're right. Sorry, Jen." Bree passed the girls chunks of bread, picked up her oar, and thrust it into the water.

"But what's my prize?" Cara asked. "You said, 'First one to the boat wins!'"

Bree rolled her eyes at Devin. Dropping his oar, he dug deep into a pocket and pulled out two small, smooth stones. With a wink at Bree he gave one stone to each girl.

Bree sighed. With long sweeps of the oars, she and Devin sent the boat skimming across the water. As they turned the rowboat upriver, the bell from the monastery downstream started ringing again.

For as long as Bree could remember, that bell had called her family to worship. From the time she was a little girl Bree had loved going to church. Now the bell brought fear to her heart.

Again and again it sounded, always with the same pattern of ringing. Bree and Devin bent to the oars, rowing their fastest. Partway through the signal, the ringing suddenly stopped.

Bree turned to Devin and met his gaze. "They're there," she whispered.

Not just at the sea. Not just spotted from the high tower. Not just coming up the river or through the forest. The Vikings were at the monastery. This was not something Bree had imagined. It was real.

"Let's pray," Devin said.

Without pausing in her rowing, Bree nodded. She prayed harder than she had ever prayed in her life. For the monk ringing the bell. The students from many lands. The monks scattered around the monastery. And most of all, for Brother Cronan.

"Do you think they're all in the tower?" Bree asked after a time.

"They would have gone there with the first ring. They'll be safe."

In her mind Bree could imagine them. The students and monks hurrying up the ladder to the opening thirteen feet above the ground. Men pulling up the ladder, slamming the door, and dropping the timber bar in place. The tower was the safest place the monks and students could be.

All three children were quiet now, but Adam's eyelids were heavy, his face flushed with fever. Bree felt his forehead again. "Lie down," she whispered and stopped rowing long enough to settle Adam in the bottom of the boat.

As she started to row again, Bree saw a thick cloud of smoke rising above the trees. She remembered the churches in the area. *Stone walls. Stone roofs.*

She thought about the monastery school. *Wood.* Bree's heart sank down to her toes. And what about the houses inside the walls and the small huts where monks prayed? The walls were woven-together branches, twigs, and clay. But the roofs? *Straw thatch.*

Again Bree remembered the tower and felt grateful for the place of safety. With relief she thought about the three-foot-thick stone walls.

The moment they reached their landing place, Devin caught the rock, and held the boat for Bree to leap out. "Take them to the shelter," he whispered. "I'll hide the boat and circle up the mountain, then back to where you are."

When Devin set Cara on the landing rock, she stuck a thumb in her mouth. Eyes wide, the little girl knew without being told that this was no game. Jen was next. As Cara took her hand, the three-year-old started sniffling.

"Shhhh!"

But Jen began to wail. Catching the little girl in her arms, Bree held her close to her chest. With Jen still sobbing and Cara's hand in hers, Bree started up the side of the mountain. When Adam refused to follow, Devin had no choice but to tie up, lift Adam from the boat, and carry him.

The way was steep, the rocks more slippery than Bree had ever known. A difficult climb, even when alone, Bree had all she could do to carry one girl and hang on to the other. Once some loose pebbles threatened to send them all into the river. Once Bree stopped to quiet Jen again. And once Bree lost her breath and wondered if she could keep on.

With each step upward, she pushed herself more. With every sharp turn she glanced back down the slope. Devin was strong and climbed as fast as he could, but Adam hung heavy on his shoulders.

In the forest beneath the steepest part of the mountain, Bree looked for the markers as Devin had taught her.

When they finally reached the shelter, Bree pushed the girls inside and crawled in behind. Devin followed with Adam. Exhausted by the race against time, Bree and Devin drew long ragged breaths.

"We're here." Bree made her voice bright and forced herself to smile. "Now we get to play another game. We'll pretend that we live here."

"I'll take care of the boat," Devin said quietly, but Adam clung to his brother's neck.

"I want to go with you."

Devin shook his head. "You stay with Bree. I'll be right back."

"Don't want to stay with Bree," Adam answered.

When Devin tried to unwrap his arms, the boy tightened his hold. "I'm staying with you!"

His blue eyes dark with worry, Devin sighed. Once Adam made up his mind, neither Devin nor Bree could change it without a big quarrel. Worse still, every second counted.

"I'll go." Bree edged toward the opening of the shelter, then remembered one of Devin's special gifts. "Tell us a story," she said.

In the dim light of the hideaway, Devin sat down and leaned back against the containers of food. With Adam still in his arms and one little girl on either side, he began spinning a new tale.

At once the children were caught up in his story. The

cold, frightened feeling left the pit of Bree's stomach. Even Jen giggled at the imaginary child who danced her way across a bog.

Bree slipped out of the shelter. Half walking, half sliding, she made her way down the mountainside. When she reached the river, she yanked the rope free and scrambled into the boat.

She was still out of breath when she sat down, facing downstream. Dipping the oars silently, she headed up the river, rowing with the rhythm of long practice. With every movement, her worry about the time she had lost grew bigger.

The smoke above the trees seemed closer now. Had the wind blown it their way? Or were the Vikings spreading out? Frantically Bree searched for the place Devin had chosen to hide the boat. Turning often, Bree kept looking over her shoulder.

Have I passed the rocks? In her fear every threat grew big, every moment large with worry.

Telling herself she could not panic, Bree rowed desperately. But everything looked different from the evening before. Then she understood why that was. *This time the Vikings are here. My brother Dev is not.*

When at last Bree spotted the opening between rocks, she slipped the boat into the hiding place. Leaping out, she caught the rope and twisted it around the stick Devin had pushed into the riverbank.

Bree was partway up the steep hill next to the river when she heard a noise from downstream. The sound came from somewhere in the pine trees. Whoever it was, they were too far away for Bree to understand what they said. But then she looked down the slope toward the row-boat. Still held by the rope, it had slipped out from the rocks to drift in the current.

Bree stared at the boat. *I didn't tie it tight enough!*

The boat would give her away. If the men weren't expecting someone before, they would now. But there was no time for Bree to go back.

Like a rabbit fleeing for cover, she scrambled up the steep slope. When she reached an opening in the trees, she again looked back.

Devin had made sure they'd hide the boat on the same side of the river as the shelter. If there wasn't someone nearby, it would be simple to climb away from the water, loop around in the wooded part of the mountain, and drop down to the shelter. But now Bree had only one thought. *I can't lead them to Dev and the others.*

Instead, she turned another direction. Ahead of Bree, the mountain grew even steeper. Climbing higher and higher, she finally paused to catch her breath. Even now, she could hear voices, two of them this time, then a muffled sound quickly silenced.

Frantic to outrun whoever it was, Bree stopped her upward flight and headed sideways across the mountain.

As the trees thinned out, she thought only about putting distance between herself and whoever followed.

When she reached open ground, Bree started across the barren slope. Soon she'd find a hiding place. All would be well.

Then as she glanced down the slope, Bree noticed the dress she had worn to school. Bright blue cloth.

Bree groaned. She had always liked the dress because it seemed to sparkle like a jewel. Now she knew it could be the worst possible color. Dropping onto her stomach, she rolled over several times. But when she stood up again she knew the blue cloth would never blend with gray rocks and light brown earth.

In that moment Bree realized her mistake. In her panic she had outrun the cover of trees. If she went back, she'd lead anyone who followed to the place where her brothers and sisters hid. Ahead lay a thundering waterfall and heights too dangerous to climb. But not far away, across the open slope, was a large rock. If she could lie down behind it—

Bree broke into a run. Halfway to the rock, she looked back. Far below, two men came out of the trees along the river. With one glance Bree saw the helmets and shields, the knee breeches with leather strips around the legs. Bree had no doubt who they were. *Vikings!*

Don't attract attention, she told herself.

Slowly Bree lowered herself to the ground. Flat

against the earth, she turned her head toward the river. Still as a stone she lay, hoping the men would pass by without seeing her.

They were almost beyond Bree when one of them turned. Looking up, he pointed toward Bree. Her heart skittered down to her toes.

Oh, Father, she breathed silently. Never in her life had Bree been so afraid. *Father in heaven, please help me!*

But the two men started her way. Bree had no doubt that they had seen her. *I can't go back. I can't go forward. What can I do?*

Then Bree knew. The only direction she could go was up.

Leaping to her feet, she started climbing again, but the way was steep. More than once, she nearly lost her footing on a slippery rock. Reaching out, she clutched a clump of heather.

Small, loose stones rattled down the mountain behind her. Bree stopped, caught her breath. If she fell on this open slope, she could start rolling, sliding—

Bree didn't want to think about it. Instead, she looked up to the top of the mountain. Beyond that, she could hurry downhill. If she got that far, she would get away.

Below Bree, the two men moved quickly, taking the steep slope as though they climbed mountains every day. Even more frightening, they talked and laughed as they climbed. No doubt about it, they knew they had Bree cornered.

Step by careful step, she moved upward. Wherever a small bush grew out of the mountainside, she grabbed hold and pulled herself up. At a call from below, Bree turned.

The men were gaining on her. Fear knotting her stomach, Bree again searched for handholds. As she reached the last bush on the slope, she heard a cruel laugh.

Anger flashed through Bree. What right had they, these lawless Vikings—these robbers, these pirates—to enter her land? To bring terror and danger to everyone in their path? To climb this mountain, hunting her down?

Desperately Bree pushed herself on, taking one careful step after another. But the men were gaining on her. With each moment Bree grew more afraid.

Closer and closer the men climbed. Filled with panic, Bree forgot to be careful. Suddenly small, loose stones slipped out from beneath her. Arms waving, she tried to catch her balance. Instead, she crashed down, slamming into the ground.

For a moment she lay there. In the next instant she started to slide. Faster and faster, the dirt and stones poured down the slope, carrying Bree toward the river.

DRAGON IN THE NIGHT

Reaching out, Bree tried to grab anything she could. Instead, the slide picked up speed, gathering more soil and loose stones. As a cloud of dirt rose around her, Bree gave up hope that she could stop. She only managed to raise her arms and protect her head.

Then, just as suddenly as it began, the ground stopped moving. Covered with dirt that filled her mouth and nose, Bree lay there, unable to move.

My legs, she thought. *What's wrong with my legs?*

A rough hand grabbed her arm, pulled at it. "Stop it!" Bree cried.

With her free hand she tried to wipe the specks of dirt from her eyes. Instead, she made everything worse.

Blinking, she struggled to see. Only then did she realize that her legs lay under a mound of dirt and small stones.

Digging with their hands, the men pushed the dirt aside. Though Bree still wondered if she could move, one of them jerked her arm and pulled her up.

Through the grit in her eyes, Bree looked from one to the other. Her captors were not men but lads about her age. When one of them pointed toward the river, Bree knew he intended her to walk the rest of the way down the slope. She also knew she had no choice but to start.

To Bree's relief her legs worked. As she stumbled down the mountainside, her thoughts scurried every which way, then settled on a frantic prayer. *Jesus. Protect me, Jesus.*

Over and over, Bree prayed His name. One question pounded away at her mind. *How can I escape?*

But the lads walked close behind her. When she tried to run, one of them grabbed Bree's arm and held up a fist. When she pretended that she couldn't keep up, the other pushed her ahead. And when Bree reached the bank of the river, the taller of the two lads took a rope made from walrus hide and tied her wrists together. Pointing downstream, he made it clear that she should start walking again.

For as long as she could remember, Bree had played in this forest. In spite of her fear, she knew exactly where she was. And now as they walked, her captors shoved her toward the O'Toole farm. When Bree saw where they were headed, her dread grew. If somehow the Vikings missed her family's farm on their way upriver, they could happen upon it now.

As much as Bree wanted to break free and run home, she couldn't let them find her mother and grandmother. When Bree and the Vikings drew close to the buildings, she grew frantic. How could she change where they were going?

Stumbling as if she had lost her balance, Bree fell to the ground. With her hands tied, she had trouble getting back on her feet. One of the lads yanked her arm and pulled her up.

Setting out once more, Bree again walked ahead of them, but now she knew what to do. Changing direction gradually, she swerved away from the farm. After what seemed forever, she led the boys beyond the buildings and the place where Mam and Granny hid.

For an instant Bree felt relieved. The next moment she felt like crying. *Will I ever see my family again?*

Only yesterday Bree had longed to visit new places. Now she wanted nothing else but to be home. To be safe. To hug her parents and feel their arms wrapped around her.

As Bree and her captors walked, one stream joined another, and then they followed the Avonmore River. The mists of Ireland fell upon them. Then the skies opened, and Bree was soon wet to her skin. But when night came, it was even worse, for the darkness settled into Bree's spirit. One moment she felt that what was happening couldn't be true. The next moment she knew that it was.

Like a bird beating its wings against a cage, Bree wanted only to be free.

After the longest walk in her life, she and the lads who had captured her reached the other Vikings. The pirates from the North had brought their longship partway up the Avonmore River. At the front of the ship a great dragon head rose high in the air. Blacker than the night sky, its fierce open mouth seemed ready to spit fire.

The sight of the dragon brought fresh terror to Bree. With one look at the fierce head, she tried to run. Her captors stopped her.

Strong-looking men with broad shoulders stood along the riverbank, facing away from the ship. When one of them spoke to the lads with Bree, she guessed that the men had been waiting to sail.

The two boys gave Bree no choice but to climb aboard. There they tied a rope around her ankles, leaving only a short length of line between her feet. Using a longer rope, they tied her to the side of the ship. Bree wasn't going anywhere the Vikings didn't want her to go.

With a final shove, one of the boys pushed her into the crowded end of the boat. With her hands tied, Bree couldn't catch herself. Falling onto the deck, she lay there, too weary to move.

Though used to climbing steep places, Bree's flight up the side of the mountain had left her muscles aching and sore. The walk of many miles had brought blisters to her feet. But worse still was the way Bree felt on the inside. Lying on the deck, she felt more alone than ever before in her life.

She and Devin—her entire family—had tried hard to outwit the Vikings. In spite of their best efforts, they had failed. *What happened to the rest of my family? To Dev and Adam, Cara and Jen? To Daddy, Mam, and Granny?*

Bree looked around. By the light of the moon she saw people of all ages. Only the old and the very young had been left behind. Scattered among them were girls and boys Bree's age or younger. Here and there, a child was weeping. Others huddled together to stay warm. Still others worked at their ropes, trying to get free.

Men and older boys had their hands tied behind their backs. Women, girls, and younger boys had their wrists tied in front of them. Bree was one of those and felt glad she could still use her hands for some things.

Like Bree, the other Irish were tied to the ship so they couldn't jump overboard and try to swim to freedom. Bree felt sure that the prisoners would become slaves, working for those who had captured them. At best someone would pay a great amount of money to ransom them.

Then Bree felt the ship move out from shore. As it reached the river channel, she heard the creak of oars. With her tied-together hands, she pushed herself onto her knees to see over the side of the boat.

Peering into the night, Bree looked for markers—the

rocks and trees she knew like special friends. Then the overhanging branches of tall oaks met like an arch above them, and darkness hid almost everything. Even so, Bree knelt on the deck, watching for a way to escape. A knot of fear gathered in her chest and slid down to her stomach.

As they sailed beyond the trees, the moon lit their way. The men who were rowing sat on wooden chests along both sides of the longship. Their long oars extended out through specially made holes in the sides of the boat. Working as one, the men moved forward, back, forward, back in steady rhythm.

Bree knew when the river widened and the Viking ship slipped past the cottages at Arklow. As they entered the sea, she felt the breeze of open water on her face. The men put down their oars, set a mast in the center of the ship, and ran up a sail.

As the moon climbed higher, Bree watched the large piece of cloth catch the wind. Billowing out midway in the ship, the square sail was a thing of beauty. But Bree had no liking for where it was taking her.

She also had no doubt about where they were going —one of those terrible northern countries where Vikings lived. For the first time Bree did not feel excited about traveling to lands beyond the Irish Sea. Instead, she wanted to live in the green hills of Ireland forever.

Still watching for markers along the seacoast, Bree saw the stony beach near Wicklow town. Soon they passed the huts of fishermen with their boats pulled up on shore. Beyond that came a great length of sandy beach. And finally, miles up the coast, Bree recognized a headland—a cliff or *bree*. Darker than the night sky, it towered above the sea.

If Dev could see me now, she thought. *Stubborn, he thinks. Like the name he gave me—a mountain that can't be moved.*

But Bree knew better. With fear grabbing her insides, she wondered, *Can I be as strong as a mountain?*

Bree felt sure that she couldn't. Now if she were Dev —if she had his courage—

The thought made Bree lonesome for home and the older brother who often teased her but always watched out for her. For one of the few times in her life, she wished Devin could take care of her.

Around Bree, the younger children had curled up wherever the length of their rope allowed them to settle. Some lay with eyes closed and seemed to be sound asleep. Others wept softly.

Is this terrible ship real? Bree wondered. *Have I really been stolen away by Vikings? Maybe I'll wake up and find it's all a nightmare.*

By now Bree's legs and feet prickled with a thousand needles. With her tied-together hands, she rubbed hard, trying to get her circulation back. It wasn't enough. Awkward now and miserable besides, she pushed herself onto her feet. Halfway up, she fell with a thud. Angry tears blurred her eyes.

Then Bree remembered. Was it only yesterday that she crept out of the house before dawn? Had she really stood on Brockagh Mountain, wanting to see new lands? If she had only known how she would travel—

Bree's tears changed to nervous giggles. Then she giggled just imagining how she must look. Her lovely blue dress covered with dirt. Smudges of dirt all over her face. Dirt changing the color of her reddish blonde hair.

Dev would find something funny, even in this. Look at the *colleen,* he'd say. Look at how beautiful she is!

Dev, I need you here. You always managed to take care of me—except now when it counts the most.

In that instant Bree felt angry. Angry at the Vikings. Angry at the way they took her from everyone and everything she loved. Angry at how they treated her, tied her arms and feet. Angry that they had changed her life forever.

Like a fire out of control Bree's anger tore through her entire being. She wanted to strike out at everything in sight —every rope, every cruel Viking, every plank upon the ship.

I want to go home. I want to be with my family. I want to grow up in Ireland and someday marry an Irish lad.

Worst of all was Bree's fear. Again she wondered what had happened to her parents. To Granny, Dev, Adam, Cara, and Jen.

Terror squeezed Bree's heart. *What will happen to me?* For the one hundredth time she asked herself, *Will I ever see my family again?*

Around Bree the night air was broken by people lying awake or stirring in their sleep. From somewhere near the front of the boat Bree heard a cough. *It sounds like Dev*, she thought, then pushed the idea away. She could only hope that he was safe.

One by one, Bree's tears slid down her cheeks. Each time she brushed them away with her tied hands, there were more.

Then, like a mighty wave, sobs welled up inside her. Bree tried to swallow them, to muffle the sound so the oarsmen sitting on the nearby sea chests could not hear. Instead, her shoulders shook with sobbing.

Suddenly, a Viking stretched out his foot and kicked her. Bree gasped.

His second kick was even more painful. Bree clapped her hand over her mouth to keep from crying out. Like a white-hot flame, her anger flared. Bree glared at the man, then hoped he couldn't see.

From the darkness came his cruel laugh. No doubt about it, he knew how she felt. That only made things worse.

Bree clenched her fists until her fingernails bit into the palms of her hands. Taking a deep breath, she made a promise to herself. *From now on, I will not show my anger and hurt. I will not show any feeling that makes them think they're winning.*

As though he could hear Bree's thoughts, the man laughed again. The evil sound sent shivers down her spine.

Forcing herself to be still, Bree lay down, but her thoughts raced ahead of the wind that filled the sail. *How will I ever hide my feelings? How can I keep them from knowing how upset I am? How much I hurt? How much I hate them?*

Closing her eyes, Bree remembered home, her mother's good cooking, Jen and Cara, and the feel of their arms around her neck. She remembered lambs playing in the green meadow. She thought of the tall trees near their cottage with the thatched straw roof.

Just the same, her tears returned. On her knees again, Bree covered her mouth with her hands and sobbed into the boards of the deck. This time no sound escaped her lips.

At last, exhausted from weeping, Bree finally lay still. The night wind was cold, her dress was still wet, and she had no cloak to cover her. There in the dark, surrounded by prisoners who were afraid to talk, Bree thought of Brother Cronan.

The kind monk seemed at least one hundred years away, but Bree remembered his words. When he helped her learn the Holy Scriptures, he said, "When you have a hard time, call up the verses you've memorized. Repeat them in your mind."

And Daddy. Was it only yesterday that he reminded her of God's special gift—His Word in her heart? "Whatever you face, if you ask God to help you, He will," Daddy had said.

Now Bree knew just the thought she needed—a verse from the fourth Psalm. For the first time she wondered about the shepherd boy who wrote the words. What was it like to guard sheep in the fields at night? To keep wild animals away?

To Bree the Vikings seemed like wild animals. The boy David seemed even farther away than Cronan. But Bree knew David's words: *I will lie down and sleep in peace, for you alone, O Lord, make me dwell in safety.*

Dwell, thought Bree. *Live in that place.* Turning her head, she looked up, but clouds covered the moon. No shelter above—only the Viking sail that was taking her farther and farther from home. Again Bree drew a deep breath.

You alone, O Lord, make me dwell in safety. Still repeating the verse to herself, Bree started to drift off. Then she heard the sound of weeping not far away.

Raising her head, Bree listened. The weeping came from just beyond where she lay. Her elbows on the deck, Bree pulled herself that way. The rope binding her ankles dug into her skin. The rope that tied her to the ship held her back. But when she could go no farther, Bree managed to bump her head against the foot of a young girl.

Instantly the child grew silent. "Jesus is with you," Bree whispered, speaking in the Irish.

In the darkness she felt a movement—the child trying to come closer. Again Bree whispered. "Though you cannot see Him, Jesus is with you."

The child's back was turned, but Bree heard the quick intake of breath—a shuddering gasp, then silence. "Though it's dark, Jesus is Light," Bree promised. "He knows you. He loves you."

Pushing her feet and elbows against the deck of the ship, the child managed to turn toward Bree. The small hands of a girl, wrists bound together with rope, reached toward her.

Bree could just barely touch them with her own bound hands. Laying her hands on top of the cold fingers, Bree whispered again, "Jesus is with you. Go to sleep."

Quietly Bree began to hum. So soft was her voice that no one else stirred.

Before long, Bree felt the small fingers relax. She heard a ragged sigh, then the child's even breathing.

Bree felt glad. *Strange,* she thought. *It helped me to help her.*

For a long time Bree lay without moving, staring up into the darkness. *For You alone, O Lord, make me dwell in safety. And this small child too.*

Then Bree fell asleep.

Sometime during the night she felt dimly aware of the boat bumping against a shore. Opening her eyes, she raised her head, then sat up. In the moonlight she saw two men come on board. Walking one behind the other, they carried something between them. A blanket?

Yes, that's what it was. A blanket stretched across two long poles. Once before Bree had seen someone carried that way. What was it called? A stretcher?

Carefully setting their feet between the people lying on deck, the two men passed close. As they came near Bree, one of them stumbled over a prisoner. The man on the stretcher raised his head.

For a brief moment Bree saw his gray white hair and flowing beard. Then, as though very weak, the man dropped back on the stretcher. The men carrying him moved to the front of the ship. Soon Bree heard angry voices.

Straining to hear, she could barely make out a few words. Whatever was wrong, it seemed terribly important. But then the longship slipped back into the water. The dipping oars blurred the voices, and Bree felt the up-and-down rhythm of the waves.

As she drifted back to sleep, she heard someone coughing. Again the sound came from the other side of the large sail. Again it seemed familiar. Rising up on her elbows, Bree tried to see beyond the sail to the front of the boat, but darkness and people hid her view. Strangely the cough made her lonesome for her brother Devin. *It's the way he coughs when he's nervous.*

Half awake, half asleep, Bree pushed the thought aside. *I'm so lonesome for home, I'm just imagining things.*

SEVEN

SECRET MISSION

In the morning Bree's first waking thought was of her family. Without moving, she lay in the half-light before dawn. *I'm here*, she thought. *But Dev, Adam, Cara, and Jen? Granny, Daddy, and Mam?*

Over and over again Bree promised herself that all of her loved ones were home. Still hiding in the forest, perhaps, but home. On good Irish soil. Able to look out on the Wicklow countryside. Able to see the mountains and the green fields where the lambs ran free.

As if she were making up one of Devin's stories, Bree imagined her family as they returned to the farmhouse. If the peat fire had burned low, they'd stir it to life. They would give hugs all around, draw close to the fire, and warm up. Set a kettle of water on to boil. Gather together at the table and look from one to the next.

And I won't be there.

Deep in Bree's heart, she felt the pain. She wanted to cry out. To bang her fists against the deck of the ship. To tell the evil Vikings who had stolen her away to turn back. To set all of them—grown-ups and young adults and children—free.

Instead, Bree heard a voice she recognized. Lying with eyes closed, she tried to decide. Who was it? How could she know someone here, so far from home?

Then the voice drew closer, as though the person were standing nearby. Through the haze of all that had happened—through her fear, and anger, and loneliness, Bree thought back to her birthday morning. *There was something about the sound of that voice.*

And then Bree knew.

Still lying on her side, she pulled her tied hands to her chest, pushed with an elbow, and rolled onto her knees. Carefully she struggled to her feet.

The short rope between her ankles held her feet too close. The rope from her ankles to the side of the boat made it even more difficult. Spacing her feet the best she could, Bree tried to balance herself against the roll and dip of the boat. Angry at how awkward she felt, Bree wanted to lash out at the first person she met.

As she straightened, she heard the familiar voice

again. Turning, she looked into the face of the lad who disappeared after she saved his life.

"You!" Bree exclaimed. "Why are you here? Have you been captured too?"

"And might I ask what *you* are doing here?" He spoke in Norse.

Answering in the same language, Bree stretched out her hands. "These men—these dirty, smelly, unwashed heathens brought me here. And you?"

The lad drew himself up to his full height. He had combed his windblown blond hair over the bruise on his forehead. With his strong body braced against the roll of the ship, he looked down on her with cold blue eyes. "Why am I here? I am the leader of what you call these unwashed heathen."

"The leader?" A knot of dread started at the pit of Bree's stomach. "You're only fourteen—maybe fifteen years old."

"Fourteen. Yes, the leader. I am Mikkel, son of a mighty chieftain."

Since coming on board he had changed the way he pronounced his name—*Mick-el* instead of trying to say the Irish *Meehaul.* It made Bree curious.

"My father equipped me with a merchant ship." As though proud in the knowledge, Mikkel stood tall. "I brought furs, sealskins, and dried fish to Dublin. I've learned to trade—"

"Learned to raid, you mean. And plunder, and set fire

to our churches. Learned to steal and rob the precious manuscripts—the Holy Bible from the monasteries. Learned to destroy our homes—"

"Stop!"

Bree saw his eyes, the set of his mouth. *No wonder his father thinks he can lead a crew of men.* But Bree would not stop speaking. "Who are you, that you believe you have the right to destroy our homes and our lives—?"

Without warning, Mikkel raised his arm. Thinking he would strike her, Bree ducked out of reach and nearly fell. As though he read her thoughts, Mikkel stepped back.

When he spoke, he lowered his voice, as if he didn't want his men to hear. "I will not hit you," he said. "But you must obey me, or it will not go well for you."

Bree exploded. "I saved you from drowning. And you —terrible boy that you are—you capture me and take me away from my home and my family!"

For an instant Mikkel's blue eyes looked troubled. "No. Not me. My men. My men took you, not knowing who you were. Not knowing you had helped me. I told no one."

"I believe that. What big, strong Viking—what terror of the seas—would want to be rescued from drowning? Pulled to safety by an Irish lass?"

Bree's voice curled around the words. Her face felt hot with anger, and her words sparked a flash of anger in his eyes.

Mikkel looked down his nose at her. "You couldn't have rescued me if I hadn't let you!"

Bree's laugh was hard with scorn. "Let me? Do you remember what happened? You hit your head. You would have drowned without me!"

Once again Bree saw something in Mikkel's eyes that looked as if he were sorry. But Bree's anger was like a fire. "I demand that you take me back. Or let me off on the coast of Ireland. Anywhere, and I'll find my way back. You owe me my life!"

But Mikkel glanced over his shoulder toward an older man sitting on a sea chest. His long hair and beard were gray white. His beaklike nose reminded Bree of a hawk. From beneath bushy black eyebrows the man's piercing eyes watched Mikkel.

When he turned back to Bree, Mikkel's face looked hard and cold. "We've gone too far. We cannot turn around. What's more, you're my slave from this day on. Never forget that I am Mikkel, son of a mighty chieftain. You obey my command."

Mick-el. Bree heard it again. *Why would a Viking have a Bible name? Especially the name of a high-ranking angel, a spiritual prince?* But Bree felt so upset that she pushed aside her wondering.

Instead, her voice dripped scorn. "Obey? I obey someone from a heathen land?" Bree lifted her chin and stared him in the eye. "I obey God, the one and only true God. And I obey you only if He tells me."

"Then your god better tell you to obey. If you value your life, you *must* obey me. If you don't, it will not go well for you." As Mikkel stalked away, even his back looked angry.

All morning long, Bree tried to encourage the children crowded around her. As the sun moved in and out of the clouds, as the rain fell upon them, then stopped, she watched every move that Mikkel made. Like the other Vikings, he now wore leather strips around the lower part of his legs.

What did he do? Bree thought bitterly. *Change how he looked so he could spy out the land?* With every moment her biggest wish grew. *If only I can figure out a way to escape.*

Bree soon learned that the man with the long hair and gray white beard was named Hauk. To Bree he seemed familiar, but she didn't know why.

Once Mikkel asked Hauk a question, and Bree wondered if he was helping Mikkel learn to sail. Most of the time the prideful lad just swaggered about the boat. Bree hated his sure-of-himself look and the way he ordered people around. Always he seemed to think that everyone must bow down before him. Does Mikkel know anything at all? Bree wondered. Or did he just pretend that he did?

Often Bree looked up at the large square sail that carried her away from all she loved. Mounted on the mast at the center of the ship, the red-and-cream-colored sail appeared to be made from wide strips of wool cloth. Once Daddy had told Bree that men from the North had sheep whose outer hairs were long and straight. Those hairs were good for spinning strong yarn. If the wool was not washed, it contained a fat that repelled water.

Ropes held down the bottom corners of the huge sail. With the wind coming from behind, the sail stretched from left to right, separating the front half of the ship from the back.

At least she didn't have to look at that awful dragon. Even now, a shiver of fear passed through her as she remembered her first glimpse of the fierce head. If they wanted to scare her, they had succeeded.

During the day, the Viking longship stayed out from the land, yet within sight of the hills and cliffs. When the sun appeared through the mist, Bree knew by its position and the land on her left that they were sailing up the east coast of Ireland.

With each passing hour, she felt more concerned about the younger children. Most had fair, tender skin that was turning red from the wind and sun. When Mikkel passed nearby, Bree called to him. "Untie my hands and feet," she demanded. "I need to help the children."

The wind had blown Mikkel's thatch of blond hair every which way. He now wore a wrought-iron neck ring with small hammers that looked like charms. His face still held that cold, angry look, but to Bree's surprise Mikkel took a knife from the sheath on his belt. With a quick slash he cut her ropes.

When they fell away, Bree rubbed her wrists and ankles. *Freedom!* she thought and glanced toward the side of the ship. *How far can I swim?*

Her relief must have shown in her eyes, for Mikkel said, "I'll watch you every minute. If you make one move to jump overboard, I'll tie you up again."

Turning her back on him, Bree tried to ignore Mikkel. She soon found that even her freedom from the ropes was better than nothing. Using any bits and pieces she could find, Bree stretched cloth between barrels, trying to shelter the children from the wind, sun, and rain.

Going from one person to the next, Bree brought water to the prisoners. Whenever she could, she whispered encouragement to the children. "Watch for a way to escape," she told one. "Work together," she told two others. "Maybe you can untie your ropes."

But Mikkel stayed close, returning when she least expected him. Then as Bree's gaze fell upon an Irish boy of about ten, she forgot everything else.

For a moment she looked down at him, wondering what had caught her attention. With sandy-colored hair and brown eyes, he had a dusting of freckles across his nose. Why did he seem like someone she knew?

Then Bree understood what it was. The boy had the

same coloring as Keely, her younger sister stolen away by Vikings years before. Barely able to tear herself away, Bree walked over to a barrel of water, filled the dipper, and returned to the boy.

He drank deeply, then glanced up at Bree. "Thank you," he said.

As their gazes met, Bree spoke softly. "What's your name?"

"Jeremy," he whispered.

"Take heart," she told him.

To her surprise the boy grinned. "You too," he whispered. "You are a truly beautiful lass."

Bree stared at him. "Because I give you water? That's blarney!"

"If you just wipe the dirt off your nose—"

Instantly Bree rubbed the end of her nose.

"Not there. Here." Raising his tied-together hands, Jeremy touched the side of his nose. When Bree did the same, he moved his hands to his chin. "Now here."

Bree followed his example, scrubbing her chin.

"And here." Jeremy touched the center of his forehead. Finding the same place, Bree rubbed her forehead.

"Rub harder," he said. Around and around in a circle Bree rubbed until her skin felt as if it would peel off. Suddenly Jeremy winked.

Again Bree stared. Then it struck her funny. The moment she laughed, she felt better than she had in all the hours since being captured. The boy had fooled her, all right. When he also laughed, Bree saw his delight in his joke.

Then as Jeremy moved to make himself more comfortable, Bree noticed his feet. As with all the prisoners, walrus-hide rope bound the boy's ankles together. But the end of one rope stuck out just enough to give Bree an idea. If she freed his ankles, he'd also be free of the rope that tied him to the ship.

Barely turning her head, she glanced around. For the moment Mikkel had walked away. Bree felt pleased. She couldn't do anything about her sister Keely, but she could do her best to save Jeremy.

Kneeling down so that her body blocked the Vikings' view of the boy, Bree reached out. "Burning up, you are," she said as she touched his forehead. With her other hand Bree worked at the rope.

Again she glanced around. Hauk was watching now. Bree spoke to Jeremy but loud enough for Hauk to hear. "You're too hot. You need more water."

Standing up, she returned to the bucket and filled the dipper. Again she knelt down in front of Jeremy. Carefully she set the dipper in the hollow between his tied hands. As he drank, she tugged and pushed at the rope around his ankles. When it worked free, she smiled.

"If we come to land, pretend you're still bound," she whispered to Jeremy. "If you get a chance, slip your ankles free and run for the hills. Find an Irish family to help you."

The boy nodded, and Bree knew that he understood. As their gazes held, she saw the courage in his eyes. But when Jeremy wasn't looking, she remembered his joke and smiled.

Pulling out the small mirror she carried in a bag at her waist, Bree held it close. When she studied her face, she laughed again. Considering all she'd gone through, she looked surprisingly clean!

Late in the afternoon, the Vikings brought out flat-bread and cheese. Made without yeast, the flatbread was baked until hard and crisp. Because it was dried, it kept well, even for months, in an airtight chest. When Bree took the flatbread around to prisoners, Jeremy slipped some of it inside his clothing.

Bree grinned at him, and Jeremy smiled. He was saving up, all right, just in case.

As the sun dropped lower in the sky, the longship changed its course to a westerly direction. Bree felt sure they were starting across the top of Ireland. As they rounded a cliff named Fair Head, she saw a large island off to the right. The Vikings called it Rathlin.

Listening to them, Bree recognized the name. *Rathlin Island*, she remembered from a long-ago school lesson. *The year 795. The first Irish church raided by Vikings.*

Without warning, tears welled up in Bree's eyes. Then,

just as quickly, her grief changed to anger. Watching everything they passed, she memorized landmarks. If she escaped, she needed to know how to walk home. And escape she would.

While passing a large bay with cottages along the shore, the Vikings stayed far out from land. Then, beyond steep cliffs and rocky islands, they came to a bay with a long stretch of golden sand. As the ship turned toward land, Bree felt excited. Maybe here, where it was still Irish soil, she'd be able to get away. As they drew close, she studied the shoreline.

On the right side of the bay, limestone cliffs rose straight from the water. Ahead and to Bree's left, the ground was still steep but slanted upward gradually. Sheep grazed on the hillside, and reddish brown bushes filled the slopes. What looked like an S-shaped stream marked the place where high tides washed up on the beach.

Bree glanced toward Jeremy. His head barely moved, but she caught his nod.

Just then Mikkel returned. For the first time, sailors untied the ropes that bound prisoners to the ship. But Mikkel himself tied Bree's hands together. With another rope he bound her ankles. Still looking angry, he tied difficult knots that gave Bree no hope of working them free.

As the ship drew close to shore, a dog barked. Sheep on the hillside scattered, and a young boy took off running. But Bree breathed deep, filled with hope. Though she had never seen this part of Ireland, she knew it was home.

The western sun slanted across the land when Vikings beached the ship near the center of the bay. Spilling out like busy ants, they spread across the beach and up the slope. Some carried barrels and buckets, no doubt looking for a spring. Others had ropes and weapons. With long strides, Mikkel moved up the steep slope with them.

The toughest-looking men stayed behind as guards. A Viking with bulging muscles set planks in place and pointed the way off the ship.

Though no longer tied to the boat, prisoners still had their hands bound and a short length of rope between their ankles. As Bree waited her turn, she stood on tiptoes, trying to see over the people in front of her. It would mean so much to find a friend or neighbor who had been hidden by the sail. But seconds later, Bree hoped just the opposite—that none of the people she knew had been captured.

Those in the front of the longship went first. Although their wrists were tied behind them, two Irishmen knelt down and leaned close to help a lad from where he lay behind a sea chest. A rope wrapped round and round the upper part of his body held his arms at his side. When the boy tried to walk, he stumbled and nearly fell. Again an Irishman reached out to steady him.

From where she stood behind several people, Bree stared at the boy.

The hair on the back of his head was just like Devin's, but she had never seen her brother so awkward. The boy was also Devin's height and build. After mistaking Mikkel for Tully, Bree wondered if she was seeing things. Who was this prisoner? Why had the Vikings been especially careful that he didn't escape?

When the lad reached the planks he stumbled again. As he made his way off the ship, Bree caught a glimpse of his shoulders and arms. It had to be Dev!

The moment Bree set foot on the beach, she started toward him. The Viking with bulging muscles stopped her. "Stay where you are," he warned.

The boy with black hair stood with his face turned away. Though rope bound his arms to his side, he flexed his hands, then rocked up and down to exercise his feet and ankles.

Bree's heart leaped. Countless times she had seen Devin ready himself for a race in just that way.

When another Viking called to her guard, Bree shuffled forward again. Out of the corner of her eye she caught a movement—someone stepping free of the ropes around his ankles. Jeremy edged toward a nearby bush.

Bree stopped, as though rooted to the ground. Not wanting to call attention to Jeremy, she turned her head slowly, just enough to see. In that moment Jeremy slipped behind a bush and crouched down. Soon after, Bree saw a slight movement in another bush farther up the hillside.

Unwilling to give Jeremy away by even a glance, Bree turned her back. When she thought he must be safe, she again inched her way toward the boy she felt sure was her brother. When he swung around, Bree gasped.

Just in time she stopped herself from crying out. *Dev, it's really you!*

Of all the people she wanted to see, he was the one. Of all the people she did not want to see, it was Devin.

EIGHT

HEART OF MERCY?

In that moment Devin looked toward Bree. For an instant, his face crumpled like a dried-up flower, and Bree knew it was his first glimpse of her. Just as quickly, Devin recovered and grinned as though seeing her across their schoolroom.

When Bree did her best to smile back and couldn't, she guessed what her brother was doing—trying to help her feel better.

With one eye on the men who guarded them and the other on Bree, Devin started working his way toward her. She, too, moved so slowly that she hoped no one would notice. When at last they stood facing each other, Bree wanted to throw her arms around her brother. Instead, tears ran down her cheeks.

"Oh, Dev!" Bree sobbed. "Ever since they captured me—" She stopped, unable to speak.

The rope around Devin's chest bound his arms, yet he lifted his hand. Reaching out, he managed to touch hers.

Bree drew a deep breath and tried again. "For a whole day I've tried to believe that you and Adam, Cara, and Jen were safe. Where are they? Were they caught too?"

The pain was back in Devin's deep blue eyes. "I left the shelter. I went to look for you."

"What happened?"

"I saw groups of men start downriver, and I thought it was safe. But when I searched for you, two Vikings stepped out from behind the trees. Before I knew what happened, they had me."

"Cara and Jen?" Bree could only think of their terror when Devin did not return.

"I told them that if I didn't come back they must stay in the hiding place until Dad came. I put Adam in charge."

In spite of all that had happened, Bree smiled. Her youngest brother could be a torment. Awful if he was crossed, he never gave up if he set his mind on something. "He'd keep them there," Bree said.

"To make sure, I told him that if he could do that—take care of two small girls—he could become an Irish chieftain."

Bree giggled. Never in a thousand years would she have thought of such a hold on the seven-year-old. "By now Daddy would have found them."

"Yes." Devin's shoulders straightened, as though allowing the weight of it to roll off. "And you?"

"I hid the boat upstream as we planned. But I didn't tie it tight enough, and it swung out in the current. When I heard voices, I couldn't go back. I knew if I went to the hiding place I'd lead them to you. When I ran the other way, they caught me."

Remembering that moment of terror, Bree trembled. Again Devin lifted a hand and managed to touch one of hers.

In the next instant Mikkel's voice slashed between them.

"Someone you know?" he asked Bree.

She had not seen him return. Unwilling to speak, she looked away. But Mikkel moved closer. "Who is he?"

When Bree did not answer, Mikkel glared at Devin. "Your name?"

Unblinking, Devin stared at him, as though not understanding the Norse language.

"I said, 'Your name.'" Mikkel spoke slowly.

Devin stood without moving. His black hair seemed even darker, his eyes an even deeper blue. To Bree's amazement her brother did not show his anger.

When he still did not answer, Mikkel pointed to Devin's chest and repeated his question. "Your name?"

Devin straightened. When his chin went up, Mikkel looked from Devin to Bree, then back to Devin, as though catching the family likeness. Reaching out, Mikkel tipped up Bree's chin.

Edging back, she glared at him, but Mikkel laughed. "You're brother and sister. It's the chin that does it. Both stubborn. As stubborn as mountain goats, butting their heads against a rock."

Bree felt the warm flush of embarrassment reach her face. No matter what Mikkel did, he made her angry.

"You're both fighters." Mikkel tipped his head toward Devin. "He kicked so hard we had to tie him up like a wild animal."

So that's it. No wonder I couldn't see Dev, Bree thought. *He was tossed onto the deck. Probably down behind a sea chest. Left to lie there all night and all day.*

Of all the things Mikkel had done, his treatment of Devin made Bree the most angry. With her entire being—from the top of her head down to her toes—she hated Mikkel. He was the cause of all their problems. The cause of their suffering.

Yet like a flash of lightning, there was something Bree knew. She held Dev's future in her hands. In spite of the ropes around his chest and arms he was rocking up and down, still flexing his feet and ankles. If she knew her brother, he'd be gone with even the slimmest chance.

As though drawing in a breath, Bree offered a silent prayer for wisdom. Then she spoke. "Let my brother go free."

Mikkel shook his head. "He's the age where he can do much work. He'd be a valuable slave—even though he's your brother." Like a thorn driven deep and meant to hurt, Mikkel's voice twisted the words.

Bree glanced around. None of the Vikings were close by. No one could hear her speak. Even so, she lowered her voice. "It's enough for my parents to lose one child. Let my brother go free, or I'll tell your men that a girl—a mere lass such as I—saved you from certain death."

Mikkel glared at her. "And you will hold this over my head the rest of my life?"

Bree lifted her head and met his gaze. "Most certainly."

The fire of anger lit his eyes, yet turned his face stone cold. Drawing himself up, he stood taller. "I, Mikkel, am son of Sigurd, mighty chieftain of the Aurland Fjord—" Mikkel glared down at Bree. "You would dare to test me?"

Without moving, she met his gaze. Deep inside, she refused to back down. Instead, she felt the satisfaction of knowing that Devin would remember Mikkel's name and where he lived.

"You who are so fierce," Bree said firmly. "You

Vikings who bring terror to an entire countryside—you will not lose face if you are merciful."

"Merciful?" In the stonelike face only Mikkel's eyes questioned.

"Having mercy. Understanding how your mother and father would feel. Don't they care what happens to you?"

A shadow passed over Mikkel's face. In that instant his eyes betrayed him.

Mikkel was the first to look away. As though he could not help himself, he glanced across the bay to the open sea.

Bree saw her advantage and took it. "How many graves do you have in your family cemetery?"

As if she had hit him, Mikkel's shoulders jerked. When he looked back at Bree, she knew her words had pierced his heart. For one instant he seemed to be a small, wounded boy. Then, like the warrior that he was, Mikkel's face again grew cold, stripped of feelings.

With a quick motion he drew his knife from its sheath. In one slash he separated the rope around Devin's chest and arms. With a second slash he cut the rope between Devin's ankles.

"Go," Mikkel said, his voice low and tense. "Escape while you can. Find your way home."

Without looking at Mikkel, Devin shook his head. His eyes upon Bree, he whispered, "You go instead of me."

But Mikkel heard. "My mother has need of a slave. Your sister stays."

"Hurry!" Bree urged Devin. If he waited, Mikkel would change his mind.

Devin refused to move. "I won't leave you!"

"You must!" Bree answered. "Please go."

Mikkel's gaze flicked from Bree to Devin. When Devin met his eyes, Mikkel spoke harshly. "Go! The choice is not yours."

His eyes filled with pain, Devin turned again to Bree. "I don't want to leave you."

"You want Mam and Daddy to lose two of us at the same time?" Bree asked. "You heard Mikkel. You aren't the one making the choice."

Knife in hand, Mikkel shifted his feet. Impatiently he moved, as though reminding them who was in charge. "Go now or not at all!" he commanded.

For an instant longer Devin stood there, gazing at Bree as though storing her face in his memory. "The Lord is with you," he said softly.

"And with you also, Dev." A sob rose in Bree's throat, and she swallowed, trying to hide how she felt.

"Courage to win, Bree," he whispered. "Jesus is your Savior, your King."

"Courage to win, Dev." Bree offered her brightest smile.

But her brother knew her too well. "The Lord will take care of you," he promised.

Bree nodded. "And you."

For a moment Devin crossed his arms over his chest in their secret sign. Barely moving her head, Bree nodded again. She had caught his message.

Yes, you're praying for me, she thought. *You'll try to rescue me. You'll do all you can.* But deep inside, she knew that even her brother's best would probably not be enough.

Devin glanced toward Hauk. His gray head was turned away as he talked with one of the men. Like a line of ants, Vikings were carrying water and sheep onto the ship. They were filling the places where the prisoners had huddled in fear.

Brushing Bree's cheek in a kiss, Devin caught her shoulders in a quick hug. The next moment he slipped out of Mikkel's reach.

Devin's first step was awkward. On the next he stumbled, as though his feet weren't ready to work after being tied up. Then, as though finding his balance, his strides across the beach grew long. Within moments he reached the bushes growing down to the sand.

Without a sound, he slipped between them. Like a mountain goat leaping from one level to the next, he headed for the heights.

Her hope still clinging to her disappearing brother, Bree watched his every movement. Near a large boulder, Devin turned and stood in full view of the ship.

As he faced Bree, their gazes met and held. Devin

raised his arm and pointed to the sky. Catching the promise of his signal, Bree felt warmed and comforted.

A quick glance told her that Mikkel faced the ship, not her. With her wrists bound and the palms of her hands together, Bree signaled back. Stretching her arms as high as she could reach, she, too, pointed to the sky.

Just then Mikkel turned around. Bree had no doubt that he understood a signal had passed between her and Devin. "What did your brother say?" Mikkel asked.

Bree did not answer.

"What did he say?" Mikkel demanded, angry again.

Her gaze still on her brother, Bree spoke softly. "That Jesus is Savior, and Lord, and King."

"He's not king over you," Mikkel answered harshly. "And not over me either."

In the next moment Devin disappeared behind the boulder, but Bree knew he would not go far. Devin would wait just out of reach, hidden somewhere in the bushes, still hoping to rescue her.

But Mikkel must have guessed Bree's thoughts. Turning to his men, he gave an order. "Load the rest of the water quickly. We'll leave at once."

NINE

JOURNEY INTO THE UNKNOWN

As Devin raced farther up the steep hill, he had only
one thought in mind—to get beyond the reach of
a Viking throwing his spear. Taking a zigzag course between the bushes, he looked for cover with every move.
Grateful for each moment of safety, he could only hope
that no one would notice he was gone.

It was Hauk he worried about most. Hauk who could
override Mikkel's decision. Hauk who would say, "No
mercy, Mikkel."

The hardened old man had looked at Devin's long
frame and the muscles he had gained from farm work.
Devin had no doubt that Hauk knew he would be a good

worker. And he felt sure that Hauk chose the best slaves for himself.

With every move Devin tried to blend with the reddish brown bushes on the slope. The moment he thought he'd gained even a small measure of safety, he felt overwhelmed by pain. How could he possibly leave Bree? All his life he had watched out for his sister, made sure she was safe. All his life she had been his best friend.

"Go," Bree had said. "Do you want Mam and Daddy to lose two of us?"

Like a forest fire her words burned into his mind and heart. Though Devin knew Bree was right, every inch of his being fought against leaving.

When it's dark I'll sneak down the hill, he promised himself. *Somehow Bree will slip over the side of the ship. Somehow I'll get her away without anyone knowing. We'll escape together.*

As he reached another clump of bushes, Devin turned. From there he could see the impossibility of his plans. Mikkel stood next to Bree, looking up the slope. Mikkel would allow no more escapes.

From the height where Devin stood, his sister looked small and lost. Seeing her, Devin's eyes filled with tears. With one quick movement he slipped behind a bush.

Dropping onto his stomach, Devin lay on the ground. As the color of the sea changed from blue to black, he peered beneath the branches and stayed out of sight.

Working like ants, the men carried one cask of water

after another, loading the longship. Although Bree seemed to look at the sea and the hills, she glanced his way often. Once her gaze stopped long enough for Devin to be sure that she knew where he hid.

As the Vikings carried stolen sheep on board, Devin's panic grew. Desperate now, he considered running back down the hill, snatching Bree from the ship, and urging her to run as fast as she could. With every plan that came to mind Devin remembered his sister's words: "Do you want Mam and Dad to lose both of us?"

With loud bleats the sheep protested their rough handling. Whenever one balked, refusing to move, a Viking picked it up and dumped it into the ship. The men were hurrying now. Even from where Devin lay, he could tell the difference.

Still hoping for a miracle, he watched every move Mikkel made. Stern leader that he was, he never left Bree's side. With the full barrels of water and the baaing sheep in one part of the boat, the Vikings herded the prisoners back on board. This time Bree was crowded into the front half of the ship.

Mikkel himself tied the rope that bound Bree to the side of the boat. There would be no jumping into the water. No attempt to reach freedom.

With long strides Mikkel paced about, as though overseeing everything that needed to be finished. As the sun slipped behind the high cliff, the Vikings pushed at the prow of the ship. When it eased off the beach, they jumped aboard.

Devin held back his groans. Allowing no sound to escape his lips, he watched the oarsmen row the ship into deeper water. When the Vikings unfurled the large sail, the red stripes seemed to claim the victory of the cruel men.

As the setting sun cast red light upon the water, Devin climbed farther up the steep hill. From the level land at the top, he watched the ship move off in the distance. Smaller and smaller it became until the one black dot on the horizon disappeared.

With his last sight of the ship that had taken his sister from their family, Devin raised his arm as high as he could. Pointing to the heavens, he shouted to the world. "Jesus Christ is King! You heathens won't win!"

The waves of the sea sent back his voice, and Devin fell to the ground. From deep within, a sob shuddered through his body. His face in the dirt, he sobbed until the ground grew wet around him.

In the middle of the night, Devin woke with one of the few headaches of his life. At first he wondered where he was. Far below his hiding place, waves lapped against the shore. The sound confused him, for he had grown up hearing both small and large waterfalls in the forest near his home. *Where am I?* he thought, still trying to come awake.

In the darkness he lay still, listening. Then he remembered. In the dusk that followed the setting sun, he had followed the level ground to the headland next to the sea. Beyond that, he had no idea where he was. While lying on the deck of the longship, he had not seen land all during the long night and day.

Now the rhythmic wash of water against shore sounded peaceful, but in that moment, Devin felt the pain. *Bree! Lost to the family—forever?*

Trying to escape the dread in his thoughts, he sat up and peered into the night. Afraid to make a noise, afraid he would tumble over the edge of the cliff, he waited for first light. Though only half awake after a restless sleep, he felt a warning deep inside. *What if someone is looking for me?*

Without a friend or protector he felt helpless and alone. Perhaps with dawn his feelings of panic would be gone. Perhaps all that had happened would become a bad dream. Yet much as he wanted his grief to disappear, it only increased.

When the first rays of light appeared in the eastern sky, Devin crawled from under the bushes where he had hidden the night before. Still hoping that the Viking ship had turned back, he looked down on the bay. No ship waited on the golden sand. No matter how hard Devin looked, the Irish Sea was empty.

Empty except for the expanse of rippling water as far as the eye could see. Empty except for rocks, and islands, and the first rose color across the eastern sky. Empty except for the pathway of light that came as the sun grew large.

Today that sun brought no comfort, just memories that hurt. If only he had gotten Adam to behave. If only he had been the one to hide the rowboat . . .

In the misery of his thoughts, Devin longed for another glimpse of his sister Bree. As if he could bring back the Viking ship, everything inside Devin leaned toward the sea. In his imagination he saw the sail grow larger as the Vikings returned. But the minutes slipped away, and no sail appeared on the horizon.

If only I had tried harder, we'd all be safe now. If only I were the one taken instead of Bree.

If only . . .

As the sun crept higher, Devin waited, still staring at the water to the north. But the sea gave him no reason to be glad.

They won't return. With the thought came hopelessness. *The longship won't come back.*

"No!" Devin jumped to his feet, shook his fist at the sea. "No!" he shouted. "It cannot be!"

The sound of waves against the shore snatched his voice away. Anger filled him—an anger greater than any he had ever known. Not even the stealing away of his sister Keely had upset him this much. Back then, he hadn't understood what it would mean to have her gone. Now he did, and pain ripped through his chest. *Will I ever see Bree again?*

Finally Devin had to admit that his wait was useless. No matter how much he wanted Bree to return, he couldn't make it happen. Into his anger and grief came another picture—his family gathered around the table, eating together. No doubt his parents believed that he, too, was gone forever.

I must be on my way.

The night before, Devin had no thought of how hungry and thirsty he was. No thought of how cold the hillside would become without a blanket or cloak. He thought only about Bree and the thin dress she wore in the open boat. How had she spent the night? Did she have any protection against the wind and the cold?

But now Devin could no longer ignore his empty stomach and parched throat. Through the haze in his mind he tried to figure it out.

Water. Plenty of that in the sea, but he needed freshwater instead of salt.

Food. When he had tried to escape, the Vikings wrapped a rope around his arms and chest, and tied his legs. More than once, Irish prisoners had crept close, lifted Devin's head, and tried to give him food and water. Each time the Vikings pushed them away, Devin had grown more angry.

But now there was something that went beyond his hatred for the men who captured him. What was it?

Then, through his confusion, Devin remembered. Lying on the deck near the bow of the ship, he had not seen the route they sailed. How many days must he walk to get home?

From the top of the cliff, Devin looked across the bay where the Vikings had come ashore. Somewhere nearby they had found a spring. Since they also stole sheep, there had to be a place to shelter them.

The morning sun lit the hillside, but shadows lay between the reddish brown bushes. Watching those shadows, Devin felt unable to move. At first he wondered if he was weak from the lack of food and water. Then he knew. Once before he had felt uneasy like this. How could the peaceful slope before him offer a warning?

As Devin struggled to think, he remembered how Mikkel left the bay. Once he decided to go, he hurried the men along. If any Viking missed the ship, he might hide in the bushes below. And he would be angry.

Dropping to his stomach, Devin crawled under a bush again. From there he watched and listened. At least fifteen minutes passed before he saw a branch move. Low on the slope, a bit up from the sandy beach, the branch was part of a bush large enough to hide a man. Could the movement be a gentle breeze, touching the branch and making it quiver?

Devin didn't think so. Devin did not know whom it might be, but he did know he was no match for an older, heavier man.

Then he saw it—a patch of red. A piece of cloth showing through the reddish brown bushes.

Staying on his belly, Devin wiggled his way back from the bush where he hid. When the top of the cliff kept him out of sight from the ground below, Devin stood up and began walking.

As he followed a path along the sea, Devin faced a new question. How far was he from the Wicklow Mountains?

He knew only that Viking ships were fast. Men who talked around the peat fires at home said that if the wind was right, dragon ships traveled almost eight knots an hour. In Mikkel's longship they had sailed much of one night and most of the next day. That meant he must be somewhere on the north coast of Ireland. But where?

When he tried to figure it out, Devin's mind blurred. Following a narrow path along the coast, he set his pace and tried to keep to it. But often he felt shaky, even unsteady. Once he stumbled and caught himself just before he fell.

"Be careful." He was talking aloud to himself now, even as he wondered what was wrong. Again Devin remembered the Irish who tried to bring him food and water. Now their faces blurred, and Devin walked as if in a dream. Sitting down on a rock, he stared at the sea. *Water,* his mind told him. *I need water.*

Coming to his feet, Devin looked for a path down to the sea. But the way between the rocks was steep, and his knees felt shaky. A feeling of danger pressed close. This time the warning came from so far away that he pushed it aside.

Then, as he started to climb over the nearest rock, Devin stopped. His feet didn't want to set down where they should. Dimly he knew he could fall from the rocks into the sea. But there was something else—what was it?

Pushing back the hair that had fallen into his eyes, Devin struggled to think. Something about seawater. Something he couldn't remember.

Sitting down again, Devin waited, hoping it would come to him. But it didn't.

The next time he stood up, Devin wobbled. When he started to walk, his feet felt heavy and strange. Forcing himself to stay on the path, he pushed on, believing that he must.

But nothing seemed real except the rocks he must circle and the strange way everything seemed the same. Once he stopped and tried to figure out his direction. Even with the sun's help, he couldn't decide which way he was going. Strangely, his feet seemed to rest on stones with six sides.

When he began to shiver Devin knew that the wind

had changed, coming in off the sea. With it came a greater terror—the sound of footsteps behind him.

Whirling around, Devin looked back, but saw no one. Going on, he told himself that he had imagined something. But soon he heard footsteps again.

Thinking only of getting away, Devin began to run. But his clumsy feet no longer worked. Suddenly he tripped and fell headlong.

HEART OF STONE

As the longship moved away from Devin and the Irish headland, Bree felt the wind pick up. Ahead of them lay Rathlin Island. The setting sun cast a red light on the white stone near the waterline.

Bree had always liked this time of day when her family drew together around the warmth of a peat fire. But now the sun's rays fell on the dragon head at the front of the ship. Like a giant serpent, the dragon towered above her, dark and fearful. In the rise and fall of the waves, the dragon went first, seeming to lead Bree to the land of the Vikings.

From where she stood near the bow, Bree tried to ignore the fierce head. Until now she had turned to her brother, father, or mother when she felt afraid. No longer could she do that. Instead, she wondered if she'd ever see her family again.

Staring at the dragon, Bree started to pray, but angry words silently spilled out. *I thought You were a good God. Didn't my mam and daddy tell me so? If You're really good, why did You let this happen to me?*

Bree knotted her fists. For months and years their family had asked for protection from the men of the North. Didn't God hear their prayers? If He really cared, He could have protected her.

Too angry now to even try to pray, Bree opened her eyes. The dragon seemed to sneer at her. A chill went down Bree's spine.

Courage, she thought. *Dev wished me courage to win. And Daddy said I'd have it. But I don't have courage, God. I just don't have it.*

Then from deep within, Bree sensed a quiet message. *"You're looking at the wrong thing."*

Suddenly Bree laughed. Of course. It was a habit of hers. And just as suddenly she knew what to do. *All right, God, I wanted to see the world. Not this way, but yes, I wanted to see the world. I don't understand what You're doing, but I choose to trust You.*

Turning away from the dragon, Bree closed her eyes. *And, Lord, if this is where I'm going to be, I ask You—I plead with You—to somehow use my life for good.*

When Bree opened her eyes again, her gaze fell on one girl. About eight years old, she had the black hair and lashes of the dark Irish. Her blue eyes filled with fear, she stared at Bree.

Making her way between the other prisoners, Bree knelt beside her. With her tied-together hands, Bree squeezed the tied hands of the younger girl. "What's your name?" Bree asked gently.

"Lil," the girl told her. As she started to sob, Bree lifted her arms, and Lil slipped inside the circle. Holding her like a baby, Bree rocked back and forth until Lil looked up, sniffed, and stopped crying.

In the fading light, Mikkel gave the order to release prisoners from their bonds. Vikings went from one person to the next, removing their ropes. Mikkel came to Bree. As he stood in front of her, she again wondered about the small hammers on his neck ring.

With a bold stroke of his knife he freed her ankles, slicing through the walrus-hide rope as if it were made of hair. Bree refused to look at him. She wanted only to be free of the hateful ropes. If she ever saw the possibility of escape, she would make good use of it.

"Not even you would be stupid enough to jump overboard now," Mikkel said, as though trying to upset her. When Bree didn't answer, he slid the knife between her wrists.

As he cut the rope, Bree gasped. Drops of blood showed red against her white skin.

Bree's angry gaze met his. "You cut my wrist!"

For an instant she saw a flicker in his eyes, as though Mikkel felt sorry. Then his cold look returned. "So?" he asked.

"So it hurt!" From a pocket she withdrew her handkerchief and pressed it against the wound.

As though it were no concern to him, Mikkel looked up at the great dragon head. Bree's gaze followed his. "Stupid dragon boat!"

"I've a dragon, all right. But it's also my sea bird." Proudly Mikkel touched the side of the ship, ran his hand across the wood. "That's the name I chose. *Sea Bird*. Because of the way it flies over the water."

To Bree's surprise she liked the name. It reminded her of the freedom she had known in Ireland.

"Six days now," Mikkel said.

"Six days to home?" Bree wasn't sure whether to feel relieved or sorry. What would happen at the end of those days?

"Six days and six nights to the west coast of Norway. But I live in Aurland—on a fjord far in from the Norwegian Sea."

Oh, yes. Mikkel had bragged to Devin about being the son of an important chieftain. Without a doubt, her brother would remember where she was being taken.

Now Mikkel pointed to a thin haze of land off to the right. "That's Scotland starboard." The word he used sounded like "steering board." The long oar that went down into the water to steer the ship was on the right side.

"We'll sail between the Inner and Outer Hebrides," Mikkel said. "They belong to us."

"Us?"

"Norway."

Bree tried to ignore the proud sound in his voice.

"The Hebrides are islands west of Scotland," Mikkel went on. "We'll go through a channel between them. I'm taking you to a beautiful country."

Bree straightened, ready for battle. Why did this boy always manage to make her angry? "I *come* from a beautiful country."

Mikkel grinned. "But I'll take you to mountains and rivers and waterfalls."

"We *have* mountains and rivers and waterfalls. More waterfalls than I can count."

"I will take you to fjords."

"Fjords?"

"Deep waterways. Some so deep that I cannot tell you the bottom. But someday someone will find out how deep the fjords are. Our mountains rise straight up from the water."

Bree was silent. She felt sure she could top anything Mikkel would tell her about Norway. But how?

Mikkel gave her the key. "You have many green pastures. Good farmland and good potatoes. Many sheep."

"Yes." Bree smiled. "We have potatoes and sheep."

Then, like a flood of water, she could not hold back her words. "And we gather around a peat fire and tell stories and laugh. We dance, and we sing—"

"But—" Mikkel drew himself up, as though this was the most important of all. "In the far north we have summer nights when it doesn't get dark. And in winter we have days when it doesn't get light."

Bree stared at him. And that was supposed to be good?

Yet without knowing it, Mikkel had given her hope. *I'm on the Sea Bird*, Bree told herself. *I, too, will fly away as free as a bird.*

To her surprise Mikkel opened wooden sea chests and told the Irish to use what they needed. A woman named Nola took charge. Taking out reindeer and sealskin blankets, she began passing them around.

While Bree waited her turn, she saw Lil standing apart from the rest. Afraid they would run out of blankets before the girl got there, Bree pushed her forward. Then, expecting a long, cold night on the open sea, Bree guided Lil toward the center of the area where the women huddled.

Settling down on the deck nearby, Bree pulled a reindeer hide over her head. Always she had taken being warm for granted. Now she just felt grateful for a covering. *Maybe it won't be so awful after all. Maybe they'll take care of us. Even be kind.*

Thinking back, she remembered Mikkel's warning soon after she came on the ship. From his lips she had heard four words: "You must obey me." In that moment Bree had not felt willing to obey. She had thought only about escape and still felt that way. But now she remembered more. Mikkel had also said, "If you obey me, it will go well for you."

He promised to watch out for me, Bree thought, trying to make herself feel better. But one question kept coming back. *How good is Mikkel's word?*

JEREMY KEEPS WATCH

W hen Devin stumbled and fell, his knees took the jolt to his body. Moments later, he heard a shout. "Stop! Wait for me!"

Unwilling to trust anyone, Devin tried to scramble up.

"Stop!" the voice cried again. "I want to help you!"

Help? Is there really anyone who can help? Struggling to his feet, Devin tried to keep going. But he had skinned his knees and was limping.

"Wait for me! I know Bree!"

Through the haze in Devin's mind, one word reached him. *Bree. How can someone in this faraway land know Bree?*

Then Devin realized something else. The voice that called him was young.

As his mind shut down, his legs did too. Coming to a dead stop, Devin whirled around. Moments later, the boy crashed into Devin, almost knocking him down.

About ten years old, the boy had hair the color of reddish sand, brown eyes, and freckles on every inch of his face. But Devin barely took that in. "You know Bree?" he asked.

"When I hid in the bushes, I saw you talk to her," the boy answered. "Who are you?"

Devin stared at him. How could someone not know that he and Bree were brother and sister? It felt so strange that Devin couldn't speak. Like a blind man who had lost his way, he stretched out his hand.

The boy caught it. "Sit down," he said, suddenly taking charge. "You don't feel well, do you?"

He asked it like a question, but he seemed to know the answer. "Sit down, I tell you."

Devin sat down so suddenly that he realized he was weaker than he knew. To his surprise he felt rocks beneath him. The flat rock on which he sat was a comfortable ledge. Behind him was another rock, then another, and another, and another.

"How long has it been since you ate?" the boy asked, getting right to the heart of things. From a pocket he pulled a piece of flatbread and held it out. Without thinking, Devin took it.

How long had it been? Devin tried to remember. His

last meal had been at home—the noon meal it was, almost two days before.

The hard, crunchy flatbread tasted something like a cracker, yet like no cracker that Devin knew. When he finished that piece, the boy offered another. Again without thinking, Devin took it and gobbled it down. Already he felt better.

"Now, water."

When the boy stood up, Devin looked around. Close at hand, all the rocks stood upright, like sticks driven into the ground, lined up one after another. But stranger still, every rock had the same shape—six sides, in fact.

Six sides? How could a rock have six sides?

Devin rubbed his eyes. Maybe he wasn't doing better, after all.

Then he looked closer and knew he wasn't seeing things. Not just one rock, or even two, or ten, but *every* rock around him had six sides! From where Devin sat, countless six-sided stones built higher and higher, as though rising toward a peak.

Maybe I died and went to heaven, Devin thought, still feeling woozy in the head. But if he had, it was a very odd heaven. And the boy who knew Bree seemed to be living on this earth. At least he was coming back.

"Can't find a spring," he announced. "Let's drink out of the rocks."

Drink out of the rocks? Devin decided he was in heaven

after all. The flatbread had been good—much better than nothing—but who was this strange boy?

Already he was lying on his stomach, dipping his head into a nearby stone. And then, through the confusion he felt, Devin saw it. Sure, and if the rock didn't have a small hollow. And that hollow held water!

"Go on!" said the boy. "We're far enough from the sea. It's not salt water."

Rolling onto his stomach, Devin bent his head over the rock closest to him and slurped. Not all of the rocks were hollow, but he moved from one to the next until at last his thirst was quenched. When Devin finally sat up, he looked at the boy and grinned.

"I thought you were daft—crazy. Or that I had gone to heaven."

The boy grinned back, but Devin could see that he looked relieved. Then Devin realized he truly did feel better. Even that small amount of food and water had helped clear his head. "Where are we?"

"Not in heaven," the boy answered, seriously enough. "I'm Jeremy, by the way. Who are you?"

"Bree's brother." The truth of it struck Devin then, like something he had always known yet hadn't known until now. Having Bree gone helped him appreciate her more than ever before.

"I wondered about that. I saw the two of you talking to that lad from the ship."

"Mikkel." Even the word brought hatred to Devin's heart and his voice.

"Mikkel." Jeremy rolled it around on his tongue. "The leader of the Vikings. A cruel lad, he is."

"Yes." If Devin had his way, he'd spit Mikkel out of his mouth.

"He let you go?" Jeremy asked.

"Bree talked him into it. She saved him from drowning. She said if he didn't let me go, she'd tell everyone."

"She would, all right." Jeremy pushed the long hair out of his eyes. "Nothing quiet about her."

"But there was something more—some other reason why Mikkel let me go."

For a moment Devin thought about it. "Fierce Viking that he is, Mikkel could have stopped Bree from saying she had saved him. But he didn't try. Bree asked him how his parents would feel if something happened to him."

"What did he say?"

"He didn't answer. He just looked off to the sea. Then Bree asked, 'How many graves do you have in your family cemetery?' Mikkel's shoulders jerked, as though he was upset and trying to hide it. When he looked back at Bree, his face was cold and hard, as if he didn't want his feelings to show. But he let me go."

"Come on," Jeremy answered. "You need to lie down and sleep for a while."

As Jeremy led him to a sheltered place in the rocks, Devin was glad to follow. The last he heard before he drifted off was Jeremy saying, "I'll keep watch."

TWELVE

THE RED SHIRT

When Devin woke up, the sun was past the mid-point in the sky. Jeremy sat a short distance off. True to his word, he had chosen his spot carefully. From any direction that someone might come, the boy would have spotted him at once. Now Jeremy hurried over.

"Feeling better?"

Devin sat up. To his surprise his head felt clear. "We need to go," he said.

"Drink more water; then we will. I couldn't find berries."

Suddenly it dawned on Devin. "Jeremy, did I eat the last of your food?"

The boy brushed it off. "You needed it more than I did."

"I'm sorry. I wasn't thinking."

Jeremy grinned. "I know. That's why you needed it. Besides, I owed you one."

When Jeremy spoke again, his voice was low, as though he could barely get the words out. "Bree helped me escape too."

Devin's eyes widened. "Bree set you free? How?"

When Jeremy finished the story of how Bree untied his ropes and told him what to do, Jeremy had tears in his eyes. "I thought she'd get away too."

"So did I." Devin still found it hard to believe that he hadn't been able to rescue her. "I'm Bree's brother," he said again, as though that explained everything. In a way, it did.

Once more he felt the ache, an ache so deep he didn't know what to do with it. But now Devin knew something. Like it or not, he had to go on, and that meant finding his way home. Looking around, he saw as if for the first time, the lumpy black rocks close to shore.

Black rocks? They had a strange look. In school Devin had learned about volcanoes. Had something like that happened here?

As he watched, long green waves washed in from the sea, curled over at the top, and crashed with a spray of foam.

The rocks on which Devin sat were a different color —grayish brown. Now that his head was clear, they still had six sides. "Where are we, anyway?"

"Well, if you ask me, we're at a giant's causeway."

"A causeway?"

"A roadway built across water. See those steps?"

Devin nodded. Though he still felt hungry, the flat-bread and water had helped. So had the sleep. He truly felt better. Almost normal, in fact. "The six-sided stones. I've never seen anything like them."

"Well," Jeremy began, "according to my daddy . . ." He winked, then put on a solemn face. Devin knew enough about telling stories and legends himself to believe that a good one was coming.

"A long time ago, there was a giant named Finn MacCool. He was the biggest, tallest man known to this part of the world. One day he built a walkway across the North Channel so he could cross over to Scotland without getting his feet wet. He set those stones in place. . . ."

Jeremy looked around him, and so did Devin. Countless six-sided stones spread out, making up-and-down ledges over a large area of the shore. Other stones led off into the sea. Now, with the tide coming in, waves crashed against those farthest out.

"Well," Jeremy said, "some say that Finn built the Causeway all the way to Scotland so he could marry the lovely Oonagh and bring her home to Ireland. But my daddy and others say that Finn built the Causeway so his rival, a Scottish giant named Benandonner, could travel over on dry land.

"All was going well until the day when Finn saw the other giant coming and took fright. Benandonner was an even bigger, more fearsome rival, than Finn thought.

"When Finn ran home to his wife Oonagh, she disguised him as a baby and tucked him in a cradle. Soon Benandonner knocked on the door. Oonagh invited him in for tea. 'But please,' she said, shushing the giant, 'be quiet so we don't wake up Finn's child.'

"With one look at the huge baby, Benandonner made up his mind. *If this is Finn's child, I have no wish to meet the father!* As he fled back over the Causeway, the Scottish giant tore up the stones behind him. He had no desire to have Finn MacCool follow him home."

As Jeremy pointed to where the stepping-stones disappeared into the sea, Devin saw the truth of the matter. For the first time since the Vikings took Bree away, he laughed and laughed again.

Jeremy and Devin began walking then, and before long, the skies opened and emptied buckets of rain upon them. Yet they had no choice but to keep on. When Devin fell, he had skinned both knees. Now he felt stiff, and it hurt to move, but he pushed through the pain.

As soon as he and Jeremy were wet to the bone, the sun came out again.

In midafternoon they left the coast to find a place to stay for the night. Before long, they came to a cottage set on a broad sweep of green pasture. The whitewashed walls shone in the sun, and the thatched roof was fresh with new straw. As the boys drew close, a dog barked. Children spilled out the door.

"Come in, come in," they welcomed. The smallest child took Devin by the hand. Another led Jeremy up the path.

When they reached the cottage, the upper half of the door was open. Grabbing hold of the lower part, the child tugged at Devin to pull him inside. But suddenly Devin remembered the greeting Dad spoke when he entered an Irish home.

To Devin it felt strange to think about saying a blessing. Yet the events that had sent him on this walk were stranger still. Already Devin felt much older than just two days before.

Standing at the door, he called out, "God bless all here!"

The woman of the house turned from stirring the kettle. "A hundred thousand welcomes!" Her cheeks were rosy from the heat of the fire, her smile as warm as anyone could give.

"Come join us," she invited. "I've plenty to eat for a tall lad like you. And you also," she added, as Jeremy stepped out from behind Devin.

"Run, run," she told one of her boys. "Get water so they can wash."

When they came to the table, Master O'Neill gave Devin the place of honor and offered the blessing.

If lined up side by side, the eight children would make stair steps from the oldest to the youngest. The child that had drawn Devin in was seated next to him. The boy's hand moved steadily from bowl to mouth, but he watched Devin without blinking.

For Devin the fish and potato on his plate, the brown Irish bread, and the mug of milk was a meal for a king. As he dipped his bread in a bowl of honey, he had all he could do to remember his manners. He wanted only to snatch up every bit of food on the table.

Then, as he looked around, Devin knew the O'Neills had given him much more than food. For the first time since the Viking raid, Devin felt the warmth of a home— of parents who cared for their children and gathered them around to talk and eat.

When at last Devin and Jeremy could not swallow another crumb, Master O'Neill pushed aside his bowl. "Now tell us why such fine lads are walking so far from home."

As Devin told him what happened, O'Neill's face darkened. "'Tis angry I am. Angry that these men from the North keep disturbing our peace. They're gone, you think, really gone?"

"As far as I know—" Devin stopped, corrected himself. "I *don't* know. The ship that raided Glendalough is gone. But there could be someone left behind."

"Oh?"

"A bush moved—"

"It wasn't the wind?"

Devin shook his head. "I waited a long time, watching. Whoever was in that bush was waiting too."

"Over the years many Vikings have made trouble. But others have come and stayed, married our daughters, and lived without trouble among us. Would this be such a man?"

"I don't know," Devin said again. Through the haze of his confusion, he remembered seeing a patch of cloth. Cloth that was red like the shirt Jeremy wore beneath his tunic.

When Devin first met the boy, he had been too dazed to think about it. Then he took for granted that it was Jeremy who moved the branch. Now Devin had to be sure. "Jeremy, were you hiding in those bushes?"

The boy nodded. "Partway up the hill. When I saw you, I climbed the rest of the way and walked around on the top of the cliff. From there I followed you."

Devin pieced it together. He remembered jumping up and shaking his fist at the sea. Then, through his confusion, he had sensed a warning, though he barely knew what he was doing.

It frightened Devin. The Irish liked bright colors, but so did the Vikings. Many of the men on the ship wore red and green. Did such a man know that he and Jeremy had escaped?

"The bush that moved was just a bit up from the shore," Devin told Master O'Neill. "I didn't see a man, but I *did* see something red. Since it wasn't Jeremy, it had to be someone else. Someone who didn't want to be seen."

"He could be afraid," O'Neill said. "He would want to know how we'd treat him."

But Devin remembered the warning he sensed. "The lad that led the Viking ship was in a hurry. He could have left a man behind. If I was left so far from home, I'd be angry."

O'Neill smiled. "You're a wise lad. Wise beyond your years."

Devin tipped his head, thanking his host for his kindness. But he could not hold back his next words. "An angry man tries to get even."

"And a wise man does his best to protect himself and his friends." O'Neill looked across the table at his wife. "I'll stay close to home for a time."

THIRTEEN

MIKKEL'S PLEDGE

In the dark hours before dawn, Bree woke up knowing that something had changed. She no longer sensed the motion of the ship. Instead, she felt the boat being drawn up on shore.

As she pushed back the reindeer hide covering her head, Bree saw Vikings turn the boom, the long pole at the bottom of the sail. After lining up the boom with the two ends of the ship, they drew the sail over three posts at the front, center, and back of the ship. Each post had a wide arm that held up the sail. From there the Vikings spread the cloth over the sides of the ship, making a tent.

The moment the wind was shut out, Bree felt the difference. As the inside of the longship grew warmer, she drifted back to sleep.

When she woke again, Bree seemed to smell the sweet, heavy scent of a peat fire. Pushing back her blanket, she breathed deep and realized that, no, she smelled a different kind of fire.

Bree looked around. Already the other Irish had left the ship. So, too, had most of the Vikings. But then Bree heard voices.

Without making a sound, she rolled over to look. Along the starboard side someone had raised the end of the sail. Two Vikings sat on their sea chests. Mikkel and Hauk.

Morning light streamed in, giving Bree a good view of both of them.

"Your father will not be pleased," Hauk was saying. His piercing eyes looked even more fierce than usual.

"I will tell him it's not your fault. You were ill—very ill."

"He will be angry with me that this happened."

"My father is old." Resentment filled Mikkel's voice. "I know better than he what needs to be done."

"No, Mikkel. You do not know better than your father what needs to be done."

Mikkel's eyes blazed. Then he looked away as though realizing he had gone too far. "I'm just doing what other Vikings do," he said quickly.

"Does that make it right?" Hauk's voice was sharp now. "Did you kill anyone?"

"No."

"Did your men kill anyone?"

For a moment Mikkel was silent, as if wanting to avoid the truth. Finally he answered. "I don't know."

"You really don't know? Or you don't want to know?"

"I am the youngest son," Mikkel answered, as if explaining to a child. "I won't inherit even one small piece of my father's land."

"Your father knows that, and so do I."

"There's not enough work to support me." Mikkel's voice was quieter now but still resentful. "If I marry someday—if I have a family—"

Hauk nodded. "Your father and I know. In the fjords of Norway there is little land to farm. And besides, you want adventure."

As though they had finally found something on which to agree, Mikkel nodded. The anger disappeared from his eyes. "Yes, I like adventure. I like roaming the seas. I like finding out what lies beyond the next fjord."

Strange, Bree thought. *And I wanted to see beyond the Wicklow Mountains.*

Mikkel's voice was respectful now, and Bree could hardly believe the change. Who was this man that Mikkel seemed to care about his approval?

"Your father put me in charge of you," Hauk said, as though he had heard Bree's question. "Your father named you after a mighty prince."

A mighty prince? Bree knew of only one mighty prince named Michael. He was in the Bible. How did Mikkel's father know about an angel?

But Hauk went on. "Your father outfitted you with this ship and the men to help you sail. He wants you to be a merchant, not a raider. What am I to tell him?"

"That one raid made me rich."

Hauk sighed. "It's not enough for me. It won't be enough for your father."

"Then I will tell you, and you can tell him—I will listen to you and change my ways."

Mikkel met Hauk's gaze, but it was easy to see that the old man did not believe him. "Can a reindeer stop running across the frozen peaks?" he asked. "Can a fox no longer be sly in its ways?"

Mikkel was the first to glance away. As though thinking it through, he stared at a spot outside the ship. Finally he looked straight into Hauk's eyes. "I'll give you something as a pledge—something valuable."

So, Bree thought, this man is supposed to be Mikkel's teacher? But is this a pledge or a bribe?

Mikkel stood up and reached into his sea chest. Taking out a package wrapped round and round in sealskin, he handed it to Hauk. When the older man took off the layers, he held up a book with a white calfskin cover.

Bree gasped and almost cried out. Just in time she clapped a hand over her mouth.

As she watched, trying to remain silent, the morning sunlight caught the precious gems on the cover. The gems brought by pilgrims from many lands set the book apart as one of great value. For that is what it was—the four Gospels carefully hand-copied by the monks at Glendalough. The four Gospels told about the life of Jesus.

Hauk traced his hand over the cover. When his fingers touched each precious jewel, Bree felt sick all the way through. How could such a holy book—the Holy Scriptures themselves—fall into the hands of such unholy men?

Inside Bree, a weeping began. She wanted only one thing—to take the precious Book from them.

"See?" Mikkel asked. "It has great value."

Value! A sob escaped Bree. *Mikkel doesn't know what he's saying. He doesn't know it's not the cover, but the pages that are important. He doesn't know that the message of this Book is the most valuable in all the world.*

And now something else bothered Bree—a wondering that wouldn't go away. Brother Cronan had planned to hide all the manuscripts on which there had been a great deal of work. What had gone wrong that this completed Book was found? And what happened to Cronan?

Thinking about it, Bree couldn't push away her scared feelings. Deep inside, she felt torn to pieces.

In that moment Mikkel spoke. "Get up, Bree," he commanded, as though he had known all along that she was there. "Get some food."

Unwilling to let Mikkel and Hauk see her tears, Bree wiped her eyes. But this was the most awful blow of all. Seeing that holy book in their hands was even worse than being taken away herself.

But then as Bree stood up, she felt a strange hope. In that quiet way of his, did Brother Cronan know that someone like her would desperately need the words of that precious book? Had he for some reason allowed it to be taken?

When Bree stepped down from the longship, she looked around. They had landed on a small island with no shelter from the wind off the ocean. Long grasses stretched away from the sea, and the rolling wasteland seemed empty of life. From what Mikkel had told her, they must be in the Outer Hebrides.

Along the shore, prisoners were gathering any pieces of driftwood they could find. Vikings had built spits over three fires, and the sizzle and aroma of roasting meat filled the air. When the mutton was ready, the Vikings cut it apart with their knives. After taking all they wanted, they let the prisoners help themselves.

Feeling hollow with hunger, Bree filled a wooden bowl and sat down with Lil. With no knife and a spoon that didn't gather up the meat, Bree ate in the only way she could—with her fingers. Looking around, she thought about every possibility for escape.

Mikkel had chosen their stop carefully. No wonder he

had untied their ropes the night before. No one would try to get away here. There was nowhere to go.

But Bree glanced back at the ship and remembered its name. *Sea Bird.* Again she felt hope. The sail still lay over the sides of the boat, making a tent. In that moment Bree knew what to do if she ever got the chance.

Smiling, she tucked her idea away in the secrecy of her thoughts. She would watch. She would wait. At just the right moment she would act. And for now she would build up her strength.

For the first time since leaving the Wicklow Mountains, Bree ate until she was full. Then she noticed that Lil hadn't touched her meat.

"You must eat," Bree whispered. "If you don't, you'll be too weak to escape."

"Escape?" The girl's voice was as soft as a breath of air. A motion of her hand took in the barren rock, the few trees bent by the wind off the sea, the lack of any house or human being. "What hope is there of escape?"

Bree's whisper back sounded fierce even to her own ears. "We will hope until the day we die."

Lil's smile spread up into her blue eyes. Watching her, Bree felt satisfied.

When the ship set sail again, the woman prisoner named Nola called Bree over. "Look what I have," she said. "Let's put our time to good use."

From the sea chests Nola had taken pieces of sealskin

that were big enough to make warm garments for Bree and the other girls. Nola even had strong needles and the right kind of thread. It made Bree curious. How had Nola managed to be the most prepared woman on the ship?

"It's something to be glad about, isn't it?" Nola said as she loaned out her precious needles. "When the Vikings found me, I was on my way to visit a friend. We always sew as we talk."

All the women needed was something for cutting the sealskin. When Bree asked Mikkel, he let Nola use his knife, but he stood next to her like a watchdog.

Bree started by sewing a garment for Lil. With straight, loose lines, it would fit over the linen dress she already wore. Since only two shoulder and two side seams were needed, the sewing went fast.

All morning the women and girls worked. Before long, Bree also finished a sealskin garment for herself. As she worked, she looked up often to watch the coastline of the Inner Hebrides. When they sailed past the rugged peaks of the Isle of Skye, Bree stood at the side of the boat. Then low clouds rolled across, hiding the mountains.

In the choppy waters of the North Minch, a wide strait that separated the west coast of Scotland from a large island, Bree saw her chance to talk with Hauk. When he sat down on his sea chest, Bree hurried over.

Close up, Hauk's hook nose and piercing eyes seemed even more frightening. But now Bree saw him through tears.

The tears were for the loss of the Holy Scriptures and for Brother Cronan and Bree's questions about his safety. But her tears also softened her view of Hauk. For the first time she saw him as he really was—a growing-old man who lived an empty life.

Bree spoke in a voice so quiet that no one else could hear. "I noticed that you have a big book in your sea chest."

As Hauk turned to her, the coldness in his face struck Bree like the north wind. Seeing his hardened look, Bree felt afraid. Just the same, she went on.

"I know the gems on the cover are worth a lot to you. But I can read the stories inside the book. Do you want me to read them to you?"

Hauk's head snapped up. "You, a girl, know how to read? I don't believe you."

His piercing eyes met hers. "If ever the book is missing, I'll know you are the thief."

As fear leaped in her heart, Bree stepped back. But then her thoughts grew strong. *Just wait,* Bree promised herself. She would watch and be ready. If Hauk thought she was just a girl who couldn't read, he might not guess the other things she could do. Once again Bree thought about her plan to escape. *And I'll take Lil with me.*

Late in the afternoon the *Sea Bird* stopped again on a barren island. This time the Vikings carried a large iron kettle off the ship, filled it with water, and set it over a fire. As the water came to a boil, one of the men dropped in dried cod.

When the fish was ready, Bree served it to the prisoners and did her best to offer both food and courage. Many of them looked up and returned her greeting. Others only managed to meet her eyes. Still others stayed inside their fear.

Already many of the Irish had become friends. Thrown together by cruelty, they worked against the Vikings in whatever way they could. They had also learned their own secret ways to help one another.

Sitting down at last, Bree ate her fill, then took more. When she glanced toward Lil, the younger girl was doing the same—storing up strength for when they managed to escape.

As the Vikings herded the prisoners back on board, one of the sailors edged over to Mikkel. "What are you going to do with the slaves?" he asked in a low voice.

Glancing toward Bree, Mikkel saw her listening. "Be silent," he ordered the man.

Bree turned away, unwilling to let Mikkel know how much she wanted to hear his answer. It wasn't hard to see that he talked one way to Hauk, another way to his men, and still another way in front of her. Which one was the real Mikkel?

Sitting on the deck again, Bree thought about the different sides Mikkel had shown. His underhanded ways frightened her. *Dev wished me courage to win, but how can I have that kind of courage?*

For years Bree had dreamed of traveling to the world outside the Wicklow Mountains. That had been her quest—what she cared deeply about. But now there was something Bree needed to face. *Mikkel owns my future, and I can't trust him.*

The fear Bree had seen in the eyes of other prisoners seemed to be catching. Then Bree remembered. She didn't have warm clothes, or shelter, or enough food. The Lord had given her all those things. In the moment that she thanked Him, Bree's fear disappeared. There was something she knew. *I don't have to be able to trust Mikkel.*

The thought surprised her. Bree let the comfort go deep, knowing that it was really true.

As if ropes had fallen off her heart, Bree started to pray. *Lord, I just want to tell You again. I don't understand what You're doing. But You're in charge of my future. I choose to trust You.*

Then Bree remembered her brother. *I wonder what's happening to Dev. Is he able to trust You the same way?*

FOURTEEN

HOLLOW IN THE ROCK

As Devin and Jeremy finished eating, their new friend, Master O'Neill, turned to them. "Now, lads, you're our guests for the night. Weary you be, and we'll take care that you are safe. In the morning you can go on with your journey. But first we'll give you a change of clothes."

Devin held up his hand, saying no. It was too much. But Master O'Neill would have none of it. "Warm clothes we'll give you. And a change of shirts. If this man should see you—"

"I myself will cut their hair a different way," said Mrs. O'Neill. "When these lads leave, their own mothers won't know them."

After breakfast the next morning she took out a

comb and scissors. Setting a stool on the hard earth out-side the door, she told Devin to sit down.

Under her hand, hair flew in every direction. As it collected on the ground around his feet, Devin grew uneasy, then afraid. Would there be anything left?

But when she was done, Mrs. O'Neill handed him a mirror. Seeing himself, Devin grinned.

"A handsome lad you are," she teased. "No one but the *colleens*—the girls—will notice you."

But Jeremy wasn't as pleased with his haircut. When he looked at himself, he scowled.

Devin kicked Jeremy's foot, shushing him to keep quiet. Then they both put on the clothing Mrs. O'Neill laid out for them.

She had taken care that the color of their shirts was different. Instead of the blue and red they wore the day before, the shirts were light brown. If someone saw them from a distance, they wouldn't be as noticeable.

When Devin and Jeremy were ready to leave, Master O'Neill gave Devin his green cloak. Devin shook his head, not wanting to accept more. But the kind man wouldn't listen. "You'll be warm in this."

A boy the size of Jeremy gave him a jacket, and Mrs. O'Neill added a rolled-up blanket. Master O'Neill went outside to give them directions. "You walked the wrong way yesterday," he said, as he told them how to go back the way they came.

Then the family gathered in a circle around them. The oldest child spoke first. "May the road rise to meet you."

The next three children each gave a line:

"May the wind be always at your back."

"May the sun shine warm upon your face."

"And the rains fall soft upon your fields."

As the family finished the blessing, even the youngest child joined in:

"And until we meet again, may God hold you in the hollow of His hand."

Feeling sure he was too old to show tears, Devin blinked. The hollow of God's hand. Yes, that was where he needed to be.

The family sent them on their way with a bundle filled with brown Irish bread, slices of cheese, and potatoes. With the sea on their left and the green hills of Ireland on their right, Devin and Jeremy set out for home.

To keep them from getting lost, Master O'Neill had sent them back to the path along the coast. Devin soon found that his stiffness from falling was worse today. More often than Devin liked, Jeremy stopped to give him a chance to rest.

"If you take care now, your knees will heal faster," the boy told him. But Devin wanted to get home and made himself keep on.

It was a long walk back to the bay where the Vikings

had come ashore. When Devin looked down on the place where he said good-bye to Bree, his angry feelings returned.

Somehow I'll rescue her, he promised himself. *I'll make sure that Vikings never catch our family again.*

By now his knees hurt so much that Devin forgot to be careful. As he and Jeremy walked around the bay, they stayed on the flat, open ground at the top of the cliff. With only a quick glance toward the bushes where he'd seen the red shirt, Devin kept walking.

When Jeremy wanted to stop at a cottage, Devin insisted that they push on. By late afternoon, he felt sorry about his choice. Soon it would be dark, and they needed a place to sleep.

Still walking along the coast, they kept looking inland for a place that would offer shelter. Before long the blue waters of the North Channel turned black. Then the rays of the setting sun cast a sheet of flame over the water. Devin limped so badly that he couldn't walk another step. And now he felt uneasy besides.

When he whirled around and saw no one following, Devin climbed a rock at the side of the path. In every direction he looked, he saw no one and decided he was just imagining things.

But tired muscles wrapped around his weary bones. No farmer's cottage sent out a welcome light, and night was upon them.

Then, as Devin looked toward the sea, he knew what

to do. Below him and not far off, a small piece of land jutted out into the sea. Water surrounded the land, but one small rocky strip led out from the shore. Was the connecting land far enough from the path so that people who passed by wouldn't notice?

Once more, Devin looked around and studied every direction. When he felt it was safe, he spoke to Jeremy. "Come on."

FIFTEEN

FUTURE WEALTH

In late afternoon the peaks of Scotland faded into gray mist. As the wind picked up, the choppy water changed into hills and valleys. Behind Bree, the large sail of the Viking ship billowed in the wind. As far as she could see, waves moved up and down.

When Bree started feeling empty inside, she thought she was hungry. Then she thought how strange that was. *I just ate all I could. I'm filled up.*

As the waves became long swells, the *Sea Bird* sliced through them, but Bree's stomach churned. Swallowing hard, she tried to feel the wind in her face. Instead, food rose in her throat, and she ran for the side of the boat.

Even when there was no more to lose, she stood there,

helpless in her seasickness. By now other Irish folk had joined her. Filled with misery, they lined the sides of the ship.

When Mikkel passed behind Bree, she was only dimly aware of his being there. "Sure, and if the lass ain't losing all her pride now," she told herself, guessing at Mikkel's scorn. Almost she could hear him. "What's this big talk you have, Irish lass? You who thinks you are so strong."

Desperately clinging to anything that would return her stomach to normal, Bree thought of Mam and Daddy, of Dev, Adam, and the girls. Of Granny, nestled like a bird beside the kitchen fire. But now Bree felt so weak she could barely hang on. Every roll and dip of the ship brought fresh agony.

When Mikkel came, offering water, she took a sip but could not keep it down. More than once he returned, offering water. Each time she took a drink, she lost it over the side of the boat.

Finally he said, "Just hold it in your mouth." Even that did not work.

So exhausted that she no longer cared what happened to her, Bree dropped to the deck. The next time Mikkel returned with water she turned her face away, refusing to open her mouth. Refusing, most of all, to take anything from his hand.

And then Bree lost track of time. The darkness of a

night, a day, and another night passed before she woke in the grayness before the dawn of another day. From far off, Bree heard a voice telling her to set down her feet. When she tried to walk, her legs wouldn't work. But two people walked with her.

On one side was her friend Nola. To Bree's surprise the other person was Mikkel. With strong arms they led her back to the sea chest closest to the steering oar.

At first Bree just sat there, so weak she could barely move. When another Viking stepped aside, Mikkel took the long handle of the steering oar. In the growing light before sunrise, he stood behind Bree, guiding the ship. After a time he bent down and spoke in a low voice.

"No matter how much you hate me, there's something you should see. Look beyond the sail off to the horizon. See the edge of the world?"

Bree saw it, all right. Between her and that horizon, waves rolled and pitched without end. Swallowing hard, she told herself she had nothing more to give to the sea.

But now Mikkel said, "Take the tiller—the handle. Steer toward the edge of the world."

Uh-huh, Bree thought. *I'd rather steer you out of this world.*

"Go on. Take the tiller," Mikkel said.

Too sick to spit out the anger she felt, Bree sat there.

"See the edge of the world?" Mikkel asked. "When we get there, we'll fall right off."

He was teasing now, Bree felt sure. At least she thought he was teasing. But then again, maybe he wasn't. More than once she'd heard that the earth was flat. Could they really sail right off the edge?

Suddenly her stomach turned over. Gagging, she leaned over the side of the ship. But there was nothing more to come. Not even water.

From behind, Bree heard a snicker. When she looked up at Mikkel, she felt even more angry. Then she realized he wasn't the one who had laughed.

"I'm sorry, Bree," Mikkel said. "I was teasing. You won't fall off the edge of the earth."

"You're sure?"

"Not between here and Norway anyway."

"So between here and what?" Bree hated herself for the scared sound of her voice.

"Not between here and anywhere that Vikings sail."

"No Viking ship has come to the edge of the world?"

Mikkel shook his head.

For the first time Bree felt better. "That's too bad."

To her surprise Mikkel laughed.

The next minute he became a stern teacher. "Move over," he said, until she slid closer to the long handle. "Look over the side of the ship. See how the tiller goes down to that long blade? That's the steering oar that turns the ship."

Before long, Mikkel had Bree's full attention. As the morning mist fell away, Bree followed Mikkel's instructions. Making small changes, she learned how quickly the *Sea Bird* responded. When rose-colored light filled the eastern sky, Mikkel pointed out the far-off line where sky and water met.

Bree barely noticed when he handed her a dipper, and the sip of water she took stayed down. After a number of smaller sips, she found she could take a longer drink. Then Mikkel handed her a piece of flatbread. When he started eating his own piece, she began nibbling hers.

Before long, Bree realized that her stomach felt normal for the first time in what seemed like years. "Did you bring me back here on purpose?" she asked.

Mikkel nodded.

"You knew that if I looked at the horizon I'd feel better?"

Again Mikkel nodded. "Some people do."

"Thank you, Mikkel," Bree said. "I wouldn't have made it."

He grinned. "I know. I'm just protecting my future wealth."

Bree choked. "Your future wealth?"

"What you're worth to me."

Suddenly, all of Bree's anger returned, and with it a fiery desire to hurt. "Not what I'm worth as a human being."

As though she had hit him, Mikkel drew back. He was surprised at her honesty, Bree knew. Surprised at her understanding of what could happen.

When he started to speak, Bree cut him off. "You say your mother needs me as a slave. Is that really true? If you sold me, you'd get a lot of money."

A cold mask slid down over Mikkel's face. "Of course."

Even his voice sounded stiff. But Bree's words were hot with anger. "And you want that price to be high. So you're not taking chances on my health."

Mikkel gave a straight answer. "My father built this ship for me. When I return, I must pay him what I owe."

So angry now that she could not even speak, Bree stood up. Her arm hit the handle of the steering oar and the ship changed its course. Reaching out, Mikkel righted the tiller. By the time the *Sea Bird* held steady, Bree was halfway up the ship.

"Come back," Mikkel ordered, leaving no room for her to disobey.

When Bree returned, he said, "If you feel sick again, look at the horizon."

"So I protect your future wealth." Bitterness filled Bree's voice.

But his eyes held hers as he nodded. "So you protect my wealth."

As Bree started off again, a storm of tears rose within her. For a few minutes she had forgotten where she was. Forgotten that the Viking who helped her go beyond sea-sickness was not a new friend, but an enemy. In the land she would soon enter, he would be a lifelong enemy.

Her dread of that world filled Bree with pain. Again Mikkel had broken her trust—her willingness to hope that even he could do good things for others.

But then Bree remembered. *I don't have to trust Mikkel for my future. My trust is in God.*

Suddenly Bree whirled around, marched straight up to Mikkel, and spoke into his face. "I don't believe you," she said. "There's a small part of you—a very small part of you—that is kind, whether you know it or not."

SIXTEEN

THE WARNING

As the stars came out, Devin and Jeremy left the path along the Irish coast. Climbing like nimble goats, they passed over the small bridge of land. Beyond was a wide plateau of grass-covered rock. On the side toward the sea, the land sloped upward before dropping to the water, forming a natural wall against the wind and the waves.

No danger there, thought Devin. *No falling into the sea.*

On the side toward land, the rock rose higher, shielding them from view. At the center of their hiding place, moss covered the rocky soil.

Wrapping his cloak around him, Devin lay down in the soft hollow. Nearby, Jeremy settled himself on the blanket given to them by the O'Neills. Lying on his back, Devin looked up at the stars.

High above him, they were coming out one by one. As the sky grew darker, the stars grew brighter. With nothing to limit his view, the night sky seemed bigger than he had ever known. Devin felt as if he could reach up and touch God.

To his surprise there was something he knew. As awful as the past few days had been, they could have been even worse.

When he was totally confused, not understanding what was wrong with him, Jeremy had found him. When they needed a place to stay, they had found the O'Neills. The family had given them a warm fire, food, bed, and clothes. When he and Jeremy needed a place to sleep, God had shown them what to do.

Often Devin didn't take time to pray. Usually he told himself that was Brother Cronan's job. But now Devin couldn't get the Glendalough monk out of his mind.

He said I was a born leader, but I couldn't take care of Bree. It's my fault that she was stolen away by Vikings.

Since standing up to the mean boy next door, Devin had known how to win. And win he did. In every contest with lads his age, Devin stood at the top. With nearly everything he tried, Devin succeeded.

Until now—when it counted the most.

Still looking up at the stars, Devin started to pray.

"I'm not a leader, God. Not like Brother Cronan thinks. A leader needs to be strong—able to stand up to things —able to win. Right now, I just want to give up."

In the next moment Devin heard it. The sound of the sea had been in his ears all day, but this was different. First a soft swish, then a whooshing like the wind rushing into a narrow space. Then the roaring crash of water against rock.

In spite of his tiredness, Devin crept toward the sound of the waves. Lying flat on his stomach, he peered over the edge.

The sea had found its way into a rocky ravine about fifteen feet wide and twenty feet long. Each time the waves rolled in, they leaped up the rocks. In the thin light of the stars, the white foam of the sea turned silver as it crashed against the rocks. Devin felt its spray against his face, tasted its salt on his lips, and knew the sea was a living thing.

When he returned to the hollow in the rock, Jeremy was asleep. Lying on his back, Devin again looked up at the stars. Though the dampness of the ground crept through his cloak, he felt strangely warm inside.

As a cloud drifted across the stars, a childhood memory drifted across his mind—Mam tucking the blankets around his chin as she whispered Psalm 139: "If I settle on the far side of the sea, even there your hand will guide me, your right hand will hold me fast."

Drawing a long, deep breath, Devin waited, then remembered the rest.

"If I say, 'Surely the darkness will hide me and the light become night around me,' even the darkness will not be dark to you; the night will shine like the day, for darkness is as light to you."

"Your hand will guide me, Lord," Devin whispered. "Your right hand will hold me fast."

With comfort deep in his heart, he pushed the dangers that lay behind and ahead out of his mind. As if resting in his bed at home, Devin drifted off to sleep.

Hours later, he woke to the sound of the sea. Though still in the hollow of the rock, he felt as if he were running from someone. As he listened to the waves wash against the shore, Devin tried to figure it out.

What woke me? he wondered. He wasn't sure, but he knew one thing. He and Jeremy needed to be on their way. Devin didn't understand why. He just knew that nothing else seemed important.

Gray mist hung over the water. In the half-light before dawn, Devin found his shoes. Leaning over, he spoke softly. "Jeremy! Wake up!"

Together they ate the last of the bread and cheese. Soon after they set out, the skies opened, and cold rain slashed down upon them. With the mists of Ireland coming and going all morning, they were soaked through. The road grew soft, and by midday Devin's stomach rumbled with hunger.

As he and Jeremy passed through a forest, they walked a short distance into the trees. When Devin sat down to rest, he looked at his shoes. His right foot was wet, and the sole of that shoe had a strange jagged tear. Devin felt concerned. He had no money and could not possibly reach home before the shoe gave out completely.

Then Devin shrugged. When compared with everything else that had happened, it didn't seem important. If needed, he could walk barefoot. But how cold would it be by the time they reached the Wicklow Mountains?

In that moment Jeremy turned to him. "Where do you think Bree is right now?"

"I don't know," Devin answered.

Then he did know. Deep inside, he felt a warning, a nudge to pray.

"We're on the way home," he told Jeremy. "Good Irish folk will help us. If we just keep walking, we'll see our families again. But I'm scared about Bree."

Jeremy nodded. "Something's wrong. Even more wrong, I mean."

Devin agreed. "Let's pray for her." Whatever was happening, he felt sure that Bree was in the worst danger of her life.

SEVENTEEN

GOD'S CHILDREN

T he cloud started as a small dot along the horizon and
grew larger within minutes. Flat and anvil-shaped
along the top, it was building in a way Bree had never
seen. When the speed at which the Vikings worked suddenly changed, she knew she had not imagined the threat.

Mikkel's commands became short and quick. "Get the
sail down at once!"

Instantly men gathered around the mast, the tall pole
at the center of the ship. Across the top of the sail, a pole
called a yard stretched out the upper edge of the cloth. A
halyard, or rope, ran from the middle of that pole, through
a hole near the top of the mast, and then dropped to the

deck. When men tried to release the sail, it would not come down.

One Viking, then another, climbed up the mast. Each hanging on with one arm, they worked together. As they tried to free the walrus-hide rope, the anvil-shaped cloud moved across the sun. Around the ship, the sea took on a gray, then a greenish black color. From a distance came the rumble of thunder.

Hot one moment, the air suddenly turned cold. Within minutes, the wind picked up and waves rocked the ship. On deck, men worked feverishly, tying down anything that could move. Already the long oars were in, lashed, and stowed out of the way. With quick strides, Mikkel and Hauk hurried from one place to the next, making sure all was in order. More than once they looked to the top of the sail.

From the base of the mast, Hauk shouted, "Hurry it up!" When neither man looked down, Hauk called again, cupping his hands against the wind. "Hurry it up!"

Still neither man paid attention. "They can't hear!" muttered a prisoner.

Off in the distance lightning flashed. The thunder was louder now and the sky green. A gust of wind sent Mikkel to the mast. Grabbing hold of the pole, he gripped and pulled with his hands and legs, shinnying his way up. Cloth whipped around him as he climbed past the sail.

When Mikkel reached the top, he touched the shoulder of one man and pointed down. Sliding down the mast, the man landed on the deck.

By now everyone on deck was looking up. As the yard, the pole at the top of the sail, swayed back and forth, Mikkel and the other Viking worked at the rope. When another gust of wind caught the sail, it ballooned out, tipping the ship starboard.

On deck everyone leaped to the other side. As the ship righted itself, Mikkel sent the second man down. Moments later, a flash of lightning streaked across the sky. In the rumble of thunder that followed, Mikkel pulled his knife from its sheath and slashed at the rope holding the sail. Strong and tough, the walrus hide did not give.

Near at hand, lightning zigzagged from cloud to sea. As the world went white around them, the tall mast swung back and forth like a stick whipped by a child.

Another gust rocked the *Sea Bird*. Again it leaned deep to starboard. As the mast dipped toward the raging water, Mikkel hung on for his life.

Again the passengers and crew moved quickly, bringing the ship upright. But even in her terror Bree had seen the top of the mast. As the lightning flashed around him, Mikkel slashed again at the rope. Suddenly it gave. Tumbling down, the sail landed on the people below. A man groaned as the yard sent him sprawling.

Vikings worked quickly to roll the sail. Barely touching the mast, Mikkel landed with a thump on the deck. Bree felt relieved. As much as she hated Mikkel, she didn't want him to die.

As the ship pitched up and down, men lifted the mast from its holder and secured it. Thunder rumbled from the heart of the deep. When the rain came, it was not there one moment and slashed against them the next. It stung Bree's face like needles, and she quickly joined other prisoners as they dropped to their knees.

With faces to the deck and arms wrapped around their heads, they held whatever piece of cloth they could for their protection. Within moments Vikings threaded rope from one prisoner to the next.

"I don't want to be tied up," Bree told the sailor who came to her. In the next instant a wave crashed over the bow. Afraid she'd be washed overboard, Bree grabbed the rope and tied it to her ankle.

And now Bree heard the praying. Men crying out to Thor, calling to the god of thunder. In the next flash of lightning a Viking held up a hammer, reaching out to the heavens. The crack of thunder that followed shook the ship.

A shiver went down Bree's spine. She had no doubt how close the lightning had come. She, too, felt the terror she saw in others. More Vikings cried out, "Thor!"

Who is Thor? Bree wondered. Then she remembered

Mikkel's neck ring. Hanging from it were small hammers. And now one Viking after another held up hammers of various sizes, pleading for deliverance from the storm.

Swaying back and forth, the man closest to Bree began moaning. "What have we done to displease you?"

"Throw the slaves overboard!" called another. Around the longship other Vikings took up the cry. "Throw the slaves overboard!"

Fear streaked through Bree that had nothing to do with the storm. Arms over her head again, she hid her face and prayed. But the chant grew louder as one man after another joined the cry.

Trying to hold down her panic, Bree looked up. Nola huddled on the deck next to her. "Pray," Bree told her. "Pray in the name of Jesus!"

From one prisoner to the next the words passed. "Pray in the name of Jesus."

But the chanting of the Vikings grew around them. Holding up their good luck charms, they pleaded with their god.

Then as Bree watched, Hauk crawled to the center of the ship. Close to where the mast had stood, he knelt. Raising his arms to heaven, he led the other Vikings in what seemed to be a prayer. But instead of the peace Bree knew when a Christian prayed, she felt a warning deep inside—a jiggly feeling as if someone rattled a trap for catching animals.

Who is Hauk? Bree wondered. Some kind of leader calling out to his gods? Whoever he was, the men did what he did and followed his leading.

Whatever was happening frightened Bree more than the storm. From somewhere in Brother Cronan's teaching came words from the Bible. "I am the Lord your God. Have no other gods before me."

When Bree started to tremble, it came from more than the cold. With her eyes wide open she began to pray. "Holy God, they see us as slaves. But we are Your children."

Bree got no further. In spite of the ship rocking up and down, Mikkel moved her way. On hands and knees, he crept like a child learning to crawl.

As he reached Bree, rain poured off his sealskin cloak and ran down his face in rivers. "Pray," he commanded.

"I am," Bree said. "I'm praying to my God."

"So!" he exclaimed. "That's why Thor isn't answering. He's displeased because you're calling out to another god."

"My God is not pleased with *you*," Bree answered.

Though the rain slashed between them, Mikkel shouted at her. "You must pray to the right god!"

"I agree," Bree answered. "I'm praying to the one true God."

"But Thor is the god of thunder. Thor is the son of Odin, father of the world."

"I pray to a different Son—the Son of God, my Father."

"No!" Mikkel cried again. "That's why the storm does not stop! Thor is not pleased with us. If the ship goes down, it's your fault!"

Bree shook her head. But the lightning flashed again, and this time she saw Mikkel's eyes. What she thought was anger was terror instead.

"My brother," Mikkel said now. "My favorite brother. He went down in the sea."

Bree stared at him. *Mikkel's brother died in a storm?*

In that instant she remembered standing between Mikkel and Devin on the northern coast of Ireland. She recalled her words to Mikkel. "How many graves do you have in your family cemetery?" As if she had hit him, his shoulders jerked. Her words had pierced his heart. And he let Devin go free.

With the wind lashing around her, Bree spoke. "I'm sorry about your brother."

"These men. I'm responsible for these men. Their families—"

Gone was the swagger. Bree saw only Mikkel's pain and his fear. Then she saw something else. Hauk creeping on hands and knees toward his sea chest.

Several times during the days on board Bree had seen him open that chest. From it he took a cloak to warm himself or a piece of flatbread. But now, cracking the cover only enough to reach in with his arm, he touched something.

On her knees Bree stretched up enough to see what it was. Through the driving rain she glimpsed the sealskin package. Inside that sealskin was the holy book stolen from the monastery. Hauk was clinging to it, as though to life itself.

In spite of all that had happened, Bree smiled. If she understood what was happening, Hauk had led the men in worshiping Thor. But even Hauk knew that Thor was powerless to answer his prayers.

Bree's smile lasted only a second. Around her, the Vikings again took up the chant. "Throw the slaves overboard! They're not pleasing to Thor! Throw them over and spare our lives!"

As though a cold hand squeezed her heart, Bree listened to them. When the voices built up around her, there was something she knew. Soon it wouldn't make any difference whether she could trust Mikkel. The other Vikings would not listen, even to him.

Like a warning, one thought pounded away at Bree's mind. *As soon as they agree on what to do, they will do it.* And it seemed that total agreement was close at hand.

"Throw the slaves overboard! Give them as an offering to Thor. He will be pleased!"

Bree closed her eyes and wrapped her arms around her head. Ignoring Mikkel, she again started to pray. Through all the panic she felt, she remembered Jesus on the cross, dying for her. Dying so that she could ask forgiveness and receive His salvation and eternal life. As her life hung in the balance, Bree knew where she would go if thrown overboard.

But then she remembered something else. Jesus calling out from the cross, forgiving people, even as He was dying.

Bree shuddered. *Forgive the Vikings? I can't.*

But the chanting of the sailors grew louder. One man after another joined in. "Throw the slaves overboard!"

Leaning forward, Bree put her head in her lap. Arms around her head, she tried to shut out everything else. But the voices rose higher, swelling around her. And Bree knew what she had to do.

Deep inside where no one but God could hear, she prayed. *Father, You know I hate these men. I don't want to forgive them—*

Bree stopped, then started again. *All right, Lord. You know how angry these Vikings make me. But You said to forgive our enemies, so I do.*

In that moment, Bree's knot of hate was gone. In spite of the rain, the cold, the lightning and thunder, she felt calm inside. In spite of every fear, she felt peace.

When she looked up, Mikkel still huddled on the deck next to her. The rain still streamed down his face and wind lashed the ship. The *Sea Bird* rocked upon the water. Waves sloshed over the sides. And Mikkel's eyes were still filled with fear.

If someone as brave as Mikkel——

In that instant, Bree knew she could catch his fear. Closing her eyes against it, she prayed again. "Lord, I'm scared to ask You for something really big. What if You want to wait with answering? What if You want something different from what I pray?"

Then, as clearly as if she were there, Bree saw another boat on a stormy sea. "Remember Your disciples, Lord? How they were tossed by the wind and the waves? They were as scared as I am. But You told them, 'Take courage! It is I. Don't be afraid.' You climbed into the boat with them, and the wind died down."

Lifting her head, Bree looked around. "Jesus, we need that kind of miracle now. What do You want me to do?"

And then Bree heard it—the small inner voice she knew was God.

"Just ask Me."

"Ask You?"

"Ask, and you shall receive."

Against the shriek of the wind, Bree leaned toward Nola and spoke into her ear. "Tell everyone to pray with me."

Bree waited only long enough to see the message go from one prisoner to the next. Then she slipped her foot out of the safety rope and started crawling.

As Bree moved away from the other prisoners, fear washed over her. The rain stung her face as with needles. Her body swayed in the wind. But Bree crawled past Mikkel. Past the Vikings who would throw her into the sea. When she reached the center of the ship, Bree carefully stood up.

The wind struck her full force, and she almost fell over. Bracing her feet, she leaned into the storm and closed her eyes. She had only one thought—to pray loud enough so the other Christians could pray with her.

Using the biggest voice she could manage, Bree began. "Jesus, in Your name I pray. In Your name, I ask You to still the sea."

With a trembling heart she stood there, waiting and listening. At first it seemed as if nothing happened. Then the wind changed, and Bree felt it upon her face. When the Viking ship no longer tossed and pitched, she opened her eyes. She watched the valleys and mountains that were waves level out. She saw the sea grow still.

Bree stared at the water. The relief she felt made her weak. Closing her eyes, she prayed again, "Thank You, Jesus."

From wherever they knelt in the ship, other prisoners joined her. "Thank You, Jesus."

A minute later the rain stopped. With tears running down her cheeks, Bree prayed, "Thank You, Lord."

From around her came the echo. "Thank You, Lord."

EIGHTEEN

LAND OF THE VIKINGS

In the hours after the storm, Bree knew that she was watched—watched more than ever before in her life. "Who is this girl?" the Vikings seemed to ask. Often Bree heard them talk among themselves.

Whenever their whispering began, she grew uneasy. God had given the prisoners a miracle. He had saved their lives. But they were still slaves. Sometimes the Vikings seemed to respect Bree. Other times they seemed afraid of her. What would that mean?

Late one afternoon, the *Sea Bird* slipped between a chain of islands. "Where are we?" Bree asked Mikkel.

Excitement filled his voice when he told her they were off the west coast of Norway. As the Viking ship skimmed the deep blue water, Bree stood near the bow. The rocky reefs and jagged coastlines surprised her with their beauty. Always she had imagined that the fierce men from the North came from a wild and desolate land.

When the ship sailed into peaceful waters, Bree saw a small settlement along one shore. Then everything else fell away as she looked up at the mountains.

Bree started to count them. She had never seen anything like it in her life.

Glancing at Mikkel, she saw the pride in his face. Bree had no doubt how much he loved seeing Norway again. Watching him, Bree felt an ache—a lonesomeness for her own country.

Then she looked back to the mountains. Close to the Viking settlement, the water reached into the land, providing a natural harbor. A variety of boats were drawn up on the shore. Some were longships similar in length and construction to Mikkel's. Others were smaller, and still others larger.

Nearby were a number of houses with grass growing from their roofs. From the sea the ground slanted toward wooded slopes, then rose sharply upward. Awed by the heights before her, Bree wanted to fill her memory with the sight of this place.

As the western sun touched the peaks, something dropped into Bree's heart. Comfort, even a feeling of hope.

Hope? How could she feel hope? This was the land of

the Vikings. The men from the North who had changed her life forever.

Hope. Bree thought about it. And then she knew.

Someday I'll get home again. Not tonight. Not tomorrow. Not next week. But someday I'll be there. I'll be with my family again.

And it will be good!

As clouds moved in and night wrapped dark arms around them, the Vikings beached the *Sea Bird*. Moments later, it started to rain. Quickly the men dropped the sail onto the supports at the center of the ship. When the wind caught the cloth, they lashed it to the oar ports.

Bree hadn't counted on that. Guiding Lil along, she stayed under the sail but moved as far as possible from the end of the boat where Mikkel and Hauk kept their sea chests. Near the prow, where the sail did not completely cover the deck, Bree claimed her spot for the night. They would be wet from blowing rain, she knew. Wet and cold. But next to the side of the boat, she and Lil waited.

When the Vikings finished eating, they left to seek out their friends. Bree watched to be sure that Mikkel and Hauk went with them. As they walked toward the houses along the shore, Bree heard them laughing. The sound made her lonesome for home.

Outside the ship, four Vikings stood guard to be sure that no prisoners escaped. Before long, Lil fell asleep, but Bree stayed watchful. When the boat grew quiet, she tied her blanket into a roll. Moving without sound, she pushed two small water casks under another blanket. When she had everything together, Bree sat down on the deck and pulled a reindeer hide around her to keep warm.

Moments later, she felt someone touch her shoulder. Startled, Bree looked up. In the dim light she could barely see Nola.

"You're going to run, aren't you?" the woman whispered close to her ear. She pushed a bundle toward Bree. "Take this when you go."

"Oh, no!" Bree whispered back. "Please—you keep it."

"Shush, lamb. You'll need it more than I will."

"But you, Nola? Come with us."

"You'll have to climb mountains," Nola answered. "I'm not strong enough, but you are. When you get your chance, take it."

Reaching up, Bree clasped her friend's hand. "I'll always remember you."

Nola planted a quick kiss on Bree's forehead. "God go with you," she whispered, then slipped away.

As the night grew long, other prisoners slept. The two guards on Bree's side of the ship began talking to the guards on the other side. Still Bree watched. Then came the moment she hoped for. When a black cloud moved above them, wind drove the rain sideways. All four guards took refuge under the sail at the other end of the ship.

Without sound, Bree woke Lil. "Shhhh! Don't speak," she warned close to the younger girl's ear.

Silently they dropped their bundles from the ship, then climbed over the side. Creeping without sound, they moved like shadows across the beach. When they reached a line of trees, Bree pulled Lil into their protection and stopped to listen.

Somewhere a dog barked.

ACKNOWLEDGMENTS

I n this time when astronauts have walked on the moon, it could be easy to forget the amazing feats of the Vikings. Think about it: For decades every American schoolchild learned that Columbus discovered America in 1492. Yet hundreds of years before he set out across the Atlantic, Vikings had traveled to such faraway places as the eastern Mediterranean, Africa, Asia, eastern and western Europe, Greenland, and yes, North America!

How did these courageous sailors receive their name? Some believe the word *Viking* originally referred to men from Viken, the area surrounding the Oslo Fjord in southern Norway. Others think the term came from the Scandinavian word *vik* ("bay" or "cove") and means "the men of the bays." Men in their open boats darted out from the fjords to pounce upon passing boats. Those who went out raiding were said to go "a-viking." In the ninth century the English used the word *Viking* to describe pirates and raiders, but not those who were peaceful farmers and fishermen in the North.

It's important that we, too, understand the difference. Early accounts, written by people who were harmed by the Vikings, picture a dark and violent history. These people, whose lives, homes, and monasteries were destroyed by Vikings had good reason to feel that way. But in the last half of the twentieth century, archaeologists have found evidence of a more peaceful side—people from the present-day Scandinavian countries who were farmers, fishermen, merchants, craftspeople, explorers, and settlers. Even as we choose how we want to live, so did people in the Viking period.

Over time, the word *Viking* took on a broader meaning. Today people still think of Vikings as Scandinavians who ruled the sea. But we also identify Vikings as loving family people, skilled shipbuilders, and amazing sailors whose voyages of discovery brought them to the New World. For many people, a Viking now describes a person with a strong, courageous spirit.

If you're acquainted with Norway, you probably recognize the area where Mikkel's longship landed. Bergen is the only city in the world surrounded by seven mountains and seven fjords. Once the capital of Norway, Bergen was called Bjørgvin from early times. However, not as early as when Mikkel and Bree stopped there! It is believed that during Viking times there was a small settlement called Holmen in the area where King Haakon's Hall and the Rosenkrantz tower now stand.

In the story you just read, Mikkel proudly tells Bree that the Hebrides belong to his country. In the late 800s Norway took control of the Hebrides and ruled them until 1266, when Scotland gained possession of the islands.

When I choose the books I read, I try to find ones that build me up. Yet I don't stop to think, *This one is going to change the direction of what I'm doing.* To my surprise that's exactly what happened with two books. The first is *Glendalough: A Celtic Pilgrimage,* co-authored by Father Michael Rodgers and Marcus Losack (The Columba Press, Dublin, 1996). I started reading in order to research the Glendalough monastery. Then the words reached into my life, and I wanted to see Glendalough for myself. Extra thanks, Michael, for answering my many questions and helping me with Brother Cronan.

I've had a lifelong interest in both Ireland and Norway, but it was Elaine Roub who truly made me curious to visit the Ireland she loves. Thanks, Elaine, for your incredible hospitality, boundless creativity, and amazing patience in exploring all those places an author wants to see. Thanks for your willingness to walk the mountains and beaches with me. Your sense of story and way with words are truly Irish!

Those of you who know Northern Ireland will recognize the visit that Devin and Jeremy made to the Giant's Causeway, which is now a World Heritage Site, National Nature Reserve, and Area of Special Scientific Interest. A big hello from Finn MacCool!

Norway is the land of my husband's parents, and a second book drew me there: *Among the Fjords and Mountains: A Summary of Aurland's History*, Åsmund Ohnstad, editor, (Aurland Historical Association, 1994). My deep gratitude to you, Åsmund, and to all the authors of this book.

My thanks also to the Local History Center in Aurland and to each of you who helped me: Ingvar Vikeland, teacher and headmaster, now principal at the center, gifted communicator, and patient guide; Åsmund Ohnstad, high school teacher, author, and editor; Frazier LaForce, also a teacher and local cultural consultant.

Historian, author, and retired high school teacher, Anders Ohnstad helped me with his writing, his warm Norwegian welcome, and his in-depth teaching about the area. Thank you, Anders, for the long talks in which you brought history alive and helped to shape my thinking about the kind of people Mikkel and his father would be.

With a thankful heart I also acknowledge the help of the following:

In the Republic of Ireland:

Clare, Donal, and Helen Egan; Tommy Murphy; Kevin Bartley; Sister Martha of St. Vincent's Center in Dublin.

Glendalough Visitor's Center, County Wicklow.

Christopher Stacey, Mountain Leader, Footfalls Walking Holidays, Trooperstown, Roundwood, County Wicklow, Ireland, www.walkinghikingireland.com. And special thanks for leading a great hike!

Dr. Felicity Devlin, Education Officer, Education and Outreach Department, National Museum of Ireland, Dublin.

In Northern Ireland:

Dawn Beckett, Mags Tierney, and Breda Dick.

The Environment and Heritage Service of the Department of the Environment for Northern Ireland and the helpful people at the Giant's Causeway.

In Norway:

The Viking Ship Museum, Oslo;

Sigrid H. H. Kaland, senior curator, Bergen Museum, University of Bergen.

Janicke Larsen, educational officer, Bergen Maritime Museum, Bergen.

Captain Bjørn Ols'en, retired, volunteer at the Bergen Maritime Museum, Bergen.

In the United States:

James S. Rogers, managing director, Center for Irish Studies, University of St. Thomas, St. Paul, Minnesota; Ann M. Kenne, head of Special Collections, O'Shaughnessy-Frey Library, University of St. Thomas, St. Paul, Minnesota.

Iva and Al Danielson, who first told me about Aurland; Millie Ohnstad, heritage tour leader and genealogical editor of *Aurland Newsletter, Past and Present;* Dr. Arne Brekke, president, Brekke Tours & Travel, and former professor of Germanic languages, University of North Dakota, Grand Forks.

Dr. Bjørn Hurlen, Lake Region Family Chiropractic Clinic, Alexandria, Minnesota, and a former resident of Bergen; LaDonn Kjersti-Mae Jonsen, Culturalist, Sons of Norway, Minneapolis, Minnesota; Sons of Norway for the resources at their Minneapolis headquarters and their *Viking* magazine.

Vikings: The North Atlantic Saga exhibit, organized by the Smithsonian's National Museum of Natural History, Washington, D.C., exhibited at the Science Museum of Minnesota, St. Paul.

Rick Wagner, paramedic and manager, North Ambulance Service, Alexandria, Minnesota; Dennis Rusinko, the Viking Age Club, Chaska, Minnesota.

Special resource people Michael, Lizabeth, Lincoln, and Davika Towers; Lisa Meyer; Terry, Arden, Josiah, and Destiny Loven; David and Anne Gran; Dee and Chuck Brown; my Thursday morning group, and longtime praying friends.

My agent Lee Hough and Alive Communications, Ron Klug, wise encourager and friend, and Kevin Johnson.

Barbara LeVan Fisher for her attractive cover design and Viking logo; Greg Call for his exciting cover illustration of Bree and Mikkel and heartwartming black-and-white sketches.

My editors Michele Straubel, Cessandra Dillon, author relations manager Amy Peterson, and the entire Moody team.

As always, my ongoing gratitude to my husband, Roy, for sharing the vision and encouraging me to reach for tall peaks and distant seas. And most of all, thanks to my Lord. Without Him there would be no story.

Since 1894, Moody Publishers has been dedicated to equip and motivate people to advance the cause of Christ by publishing evangelical Christian literature and other media for all ages, around the world. Because we are a ministry of the Moody Bible Institute of Chicago, a portion of the proceeds from the sale of this book go to train the next generation of Christian leaders.

If we may serve you in any way in your spiritual journey toward understanding Christ and the Christian life, please contact us at www.moodypublishers.com.

"All Scripture is God-breathed and is useful for teaching, rebuking, correcting and training in righteousness, so that the man of God may be thoroughly equipped for every good work."
—2 TIMOTHY 3:16, 17

MOODY
PUBLISHERS

THE NAME YOU CAN TRUST®

Mystery of the Silver Coins

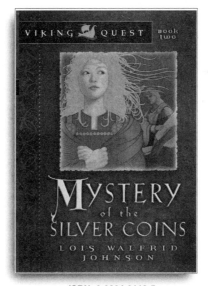

ISBN: 0-8024-3113-5

In this second installment of the Viking Quest series, Bree finds herself in a physical and spiritual battle for survival in the homeland of her Viking captors. With another young slave named Lil, she makes a daring escape from the ship as soon as it reaches harbor in Norway. The girls hide in the woods as Mikkel and his Viking sailors begin a relentless search, certain that Bree is responsible for a missing bag of silver coins.

Bree must face her unwillingness to forgive the Vikings and Mikkel, the Viking prince who captured Bree, begins to wonder: Is the god of these Irish Christians really more powerful than our own Viking gods?

MOODY
PUBLISHERS

THE NAME YOU CAN TRUST.

1-800-678-6928 www.MoodyPublishers.com

RAIDERS FROM THE SEA TEAM

ACQUIRING EDITOR:
Michele Straubel

COPY EDITOR:
Cassandra Dillon

BACK COVER COPY:
Laura Pokrzywa

COVER DESIGN:
Barb Fisher, LeVan Fisher Design

TEXT ILUSTRATIONS:
Greg Call

INTERIOR DESIGN:
Ragont Design

PRINTING AND BINDING:
Bethany Press International

The typeface for the text of this book is
Centaur MT